Henry F. Randolph

The Book of Latter-Day Ballads (1858-1888)

Henry F. Randolph

The Book of Latter-Day Ballads (1858-1888)

ISBN/EAN:

Printed in Europe, USA, Canada, Australia, Japan

Cover: Foto ©Andreas Hilbeck / pixelio.de

More available books at **www.hansebooks.com**

THE BOOK

OF

LATTER–DAY BALLADS.

THE BOOK

OF

LATTER-DAY BALLADS.

(1858–1888.)

SELECTED AND ARRANGED BY

HENRY F. RANDOLPH,

EDITOR OF 'FIFTY YEARS OF ENGLISH SONG.'

NEW YORK:
ANSON D. F. RANDOLPH & CO.

University Press:

JOHN WILSON AND SON, CAMBRIDGE.

UNTO

J. H. F-R.

THIS VOLUME IS INSCRIBED.

PREFACE.

PROFESSOR SEELEY has recently remarked that worth
and brevity are the two things necessary to insure im-
mortality to any literary production. The latter of these
two qualifications belongs peculiarly to the ballad, and it
is not therefore strange that good ballads have outlived
other equally meritorious but more pretentious poetry.
Of the old ballad poetry there are many excellent edi-
tions, notably that edited by Mr. Allingham and published in the 'Golden Treasury' series. Mr. Stoddard,
in his 'Ballads and Romances,' has included not only
the older and modern authors, but a species of composi-
tion which, as the title of the volume implies, does not
come under the head of ballad poetry. The present
volume is intended to occupy a place of its own, in that
it is devoted exclusively to ballads, and includes only
those which have been published within the last thirty
years (1858–1888).

It may be a matter of surprise to those who have not
had the time to form an acquaintance with contemporary

verse, to discover how many excellent ballads have been written during that period. The volume published by Lord Tennyson in 1880 contained such excellent work in this direction as forever to silence those captious critics who were complaining that the Laureate's verse sacrificed strength to finish. 'The King's Tragedy,' by Mr. D. G. Rossetti, has been pronounced 'the finest ballad of modern times;' and even those who might dissent from such an unqualified opinion will accord high praise to the strength and beauty of the lines. It is a pity that an age capable of producing such good work has not produced even still more. The many affectations which have crept into current verse — notably the revival of obsolete French forms — ought to be a matter of regret, if for no other reason than that they seem to be destructive of the development of those more virile qualities which are essential to a good ballad.

While accepting the simple definition of a ballad, that it should be in rhyme and possess vigorous and dramatic action, I have been influenced in the choice of subjects only to the extent of avoiding the selection of two ballads which have the same subject. The one exception allowed to this rule is the 'Ballad of the Thulian Nurse' and the 'Ballad of Isobel,' both of which have for their subject the beautiful legend of Hallowe'en; but the treatment in each is so different as to avoid anything like repetition. By the observance of this rule a large variety of subjects has been secured, from the theological doctrine of the final restoration of all souls, which forms the *motif* in the ' Ballad of Judas Iscariot,' to a horse-race or boat-race. Ballads, in fact, may be broadly divided into two classes, — the one, in which both subject and treatment contribute to the dignity of the ballad ; the other, in which the treatment lends dignity to what is in itself a more or less undignified subject. Instances of the former class are too numerous to need specification. An excellent illustration of the latter class is furnished by the ' Doncaster St. Leger.' Nothing, at first sight, could seem less suited to the dignity required in a true ballad than a horse-race ; but Sir Francis Doyle has in vigorous verse raised so commonplace a subject to the level of the truly dramatic by expanding the thought expressed in his own lines : —

> ' And during all that anxious time
> (Sneer as it suits you at my rhyme)
> The earnestness became sublime ;
> Common and trite as is the scene,
> At once so thrilling and so mean,
> To him who strives his heart to scan,
> And feels the brotherhood of man,
> That needs *must* be a mighty minute,
> When a crowd has but one soul within it.'

Humorous verse has been rigorously excluded, — a rule of easy observance, as there are few humorous ballads which deserve on their own merits anything better than an ephemeral existence. One need not be guilty of the fashionable sin of pessimism, to detect in the best modern poetry what Mr. Matthew Arnold has so finely called ' the eternal note of sadness.' In ballad poetry especially, it is only the grave and serious, not infrequently rising to the tragic, which commands more than a fleeting attention.

As the object of the present selection is to indicate the growth and extent of English and American ballad literature during the last thirty years, no author has been allotted more than a single selection. The ballads have been arranged in chronological order, and their date of publication has been fixed by their first appearance in book form, without reference to their prior appearance in newspaper or magazine. Fugitive ballads — of which there are many excellent ones — have for this reason been excluded.

I must express my regret that the present volume very imperfectly represents the work of American poets. Many authors are omitted entirely, while others are represented by selections which I am sadly conscious is not their best work. In excuse for this defect, I can only plead the unwillingness on the part of various publishers to grant me the necessary permission to use pieces of which they owned the copyright.

HENRY F-RANDOLPH.

GREY-NOOK. LAKE GEORGE,
September 14, 1888.

PUBLISHERS' NOTE.

The Publishers of THE BOOK OF LATTER-DAY BAL-
LADS *acknowledge the permission of Messrs. Houghton,
Mifflin, & Co. to use the poems of Mr. James Russell
Lowell, Mr. Edmund Clarence Stedman, Mr. John Hay,
Mr. John Greenleaf Whittier, Mr. Francis Bret Harte,
and Mrs. Margaret J. Preston; that of Messrs. Charles
Scribner's Sons to use the poems of Mr. Richard Henry
Stoddard, Mr. Sidney Lanier, and Mr. A. C. Gordon;
that of Messrs. Cupples & Hurd to use the selection by
Miss Louise Imogen Guiney. They also desire to acknowl-
edge the specific permission accorded by the following
authors: Messrs. E. C. Stedman and John Hay, and
Mrs. Margaret J. Preston.*

CONTENTS.

		PAGE
THE HAYSTACK IN THE FLOODS		1
SIR RICHARD GRENVILLE'S LAST FIGHT		8
THE FORCED RECRUIT		13
THE LOVE-CHILD		15
THE COURTIN'		17
WILLY GILLILAND		21
BALLAD OF THE THULIAN NURSE		27
THE DONCASTER ST. LEGER		31
WINSTANLEY		39
THE MASS FOR THE DEAD		51
THE DOORSTEP		57
JESSIE CAMERON		59
A WOMAN'S LOVE		64
IN SCHOOL-DAYS		66
A STORY OF NAPLES		68
DICKENS IN CAMP		78
THE DEATH OF TH' OWD SQUIRE		80
BEFORE SEDAN		86
THE BALLAD OF JUDAS ISCARIOT		88
WOODSTOCK MAZE		96
HAJARLIS		101

LATTER–DAY BALLADS.

By *William Morris.*

THE HAYSTACK IN THE FLOODS.

HAD she come all the way for this,
To part at last without a kiss?
Yea, had she borne the dirt and rain
That her own eyes might see him slain
Beside the haystack in the floods?

Along the dripping leafless woods,
The stirrup touching either shoe,
She rode astride as troopers do,
With kirtle kilted to her knee,
To which the mud splashed wretchedly;
And the wet dripped from every tree
Upon her head and heavy hair,
And on her eyelids broad and fair;
The tears and rain ran down her face.
By fits and starts they rode apace,
And very often was his place
Far off from her: he had to ride

Ahead, to see what might betide
When the roads crossed; and sometimes, when
There rose a murmuring from his men,
Had to turn back with promises.
Ah, me! she had but little ease;
And often for pure doubt and dread
She sobbed, made giddy in the head
By the swift riding; while, for cold,
Her slender fingers scarce could hold
The wet reins; yea, and scarcely too
She felt the foot within her shoe
Against the stirrup: all for this,
To part at last without a kiss
Beside the haystack in the floods.

For when they neared that old soaked hay,
They saw across the only way
That Judas, Godmar, and the three
Red running lions dismally
Grinned from his pennon, under which,
In one straight line along the ditch,
They counted thirty heads.

      So then,
While Robert turned round to his men,
She saw at once the wretched end,
And stooping down tried hard to rend
Her coif the wrong way from her head,
And hid her eyes; while Robert said:
'Nay, love, 't is scarcely two to one,
At Poictiers where we made them run

So fast: why, sweet my love, good cheer,
The Gascon frontier is so near,
Nought after this.'

     But, ' O,' she said,
' My God ! my God ! I have to tread
The long way back without you : then
The court at Paris ; those six men ;
The gratings of the Chatelet ;
The swift Seine on some rainy day
Like this, and people standing by
And laughing, while my weak hands try
To recollect how strong men swim.
All this, or else a life with him,
For which I should be damned at last.
Would God that this next hour were past ! '

He answered not, but cried his cry,
' St. George for Marny ! ' cheerily,
And laid his hand upon her rein.
Alas ! no man of all his train
Gave back that cheery cry again ;
And while for rage his thumb beat fast
Upon his sword-hilts, some one cast
About his neck a kerchief long,
And bound him.

    Then they went along
To Godmar ; who said : ' Now, Jehane,
Your lover's life is on the wane
So fast, that, if this very hour

You yield not as my paramour,
He will not see the rain leave off —
Nay, keep your tongue from gibe and scoff,
Sir Robert, or I slay you now.'

She laid her hand upon her brow,
Then gazed upon the palm, as though
She thought her forehead bled, and — ' No,'
She said, and turned her head away,
As there were nothing else to say,
And everything were settled.   Red
Grew Godmar's face from chin to head:
' Jehane, on yonder hill there stands
My castle, guarding well my lands:
What hinders me from taking you,
And doing that I list to do
To your fair wilful body, while
Your knight lies dead ? '

                          A wicked smile
Wrinkled her face, her lips grew thin,
A long way out she thrust her chin:
' You know that I should strangle you
While you were sleeping; or bite through
Your throat, by God's help — ah ! ' she said,
' Lord Jesus, pity your poor maid !
For in such wise they hem me in,
I cannot choose but sin and sin,
Whatever happens : yet I think
They could not make me eat or drink,
And so should I just reach my rest.'

' Nay, if you do not my behest,
O Jehane ! though I love you well,'
Said Godmar, ' would I fail to tell
All that I know —' ' Foul lies !' she said.
' Eh ! lies, my Jehane?   By God's head,
At Paris folks would deem them true !
Do you know, Jehane, they cry for you.
" Jehane the brown ! Jehane the brown !
Give us Jehane to burn or drown ! "
Eh — gag me, Robert ! — sweet my friend,
This were indeed a piteous end
For those long fingers, and long feet,
And long neck, and smooth shoulders sweet, —
An end that few men would forget
That saw it.   So, an hour yet :
Consider, Jehane, which to take
Of life or death !'

                    So, scarce awake,
Dismounting, did she leave that place,
And totter some yards : with her face
Turned upward to the sky she lay,
Her head on a wet heap of hay,
And fell asleep ; and while she slept,
And did not dream, the minutes crept
Round to the twelve again ; but she,
Being waked at last, sighed quietly,
And strangely childlike came, and said,
' I will not.'   Straightway Godmar's head,
As though it hung on strong wires, turned
Most sharply round, and his face burned.

For Robert — both his eyes were dry;
He could not weep, but gloomily
He seemed to watch the rain; yea, too,
His lips were firm; he tried once more
To touch her lips; she reached out, sore
And vain desire so tortured them,
The poor gray lips, and now the hem
Of his sleeve brushed them.

                With a start
Up Godmar rose, thrust them apart;
From Robert's throat he loosed the bands
Of silk and mail; with empty hands
Held out, she stood and gazed, and saw
The long bright blade without a flaw
Glide out from Godmar's sheath, his hand
In Robert's hair; she saw him bend
Back Robert's head; she saw him send
The thin steel down. The blow told well;
Right backward the knight Robert fell,
And moaned as dogs do, being half dead,
Unwitting, as I deem; so then
Godmar turned grinning to his men,
Who ran, some five or six, and beat
His head to pieces at their feet.

Then Godmar turned again and said:
'So, Jehane, the first fitte is read!
Take note, my lady, that your way
Lies backward to the Chatelet!'

She shook her head and gazed awhile
At her cold hands with a rueful smile,
As though this thing had made her mad.

This was the parting that they had
Beside the haystack in the floods.

By Gerald Massey.

SIR RICHARD GRENVILLE'S LAST FIGHT.

OUR second Richard Lion Heart,
  In days of Great Queen Bess,
He did this deed of righteous rage,
  And true old nobleness;
With wrath heroic that was nurst
To bear the fiercest battle-burst,
When willing foes should wreak their worst.

Signalled the English Admiral,
  'Weigh or cut anchors.'   For
A Spanish fleet bore down, in all
  The majesty of war,
Athwart our tack for many a mile,
As there we lay off Florez Isle,
With crews half sick, all tired of toil.

Eleven of our twelve ships escaped;
  Sir Richard stood alone!
Though they were three-and-fifty sail, —
  A hundred men to one, —
The old sea rover would not run,
So long as he had man or gun;
But he could die when all was done.

'The Devil's broken loose, my lads,
   In shape of Popish Spain;
And we must sink him in the sea,
   Or hound him home again.
Now, you old sea-dogs, show your paws!
Have at them tooth and nail and claws!'
And then his long, bright blade he draws.

The deck was cleared, the boatswain blew;
   The grim sea-lions stand;
The death-fires lit in every eye,
   The burning match in hand.
With mail of glorious intent
All hearts were clad; and in they went,
A force that cut through where 't was sent.

'Push home, my hardy pikemen,
   For we play a desperate part;
To-day, my gunners, let them feel
   The pulse of England's heart!
They shall remember long that we
Once lived; and think how shamefully
We shook them, — one to fifty-three!'

With face of one who cheerly goes
   To meet his doom that day,
Sir Richard sprang upon his foes;
   The foremost gave him way:
His round shot smashed them through and through.
The great white splinters fiercely flew,
And madder grew his fighting few.

They clasp the little ship Revenge
   As in the arms of fire;
They run aboard her, six at once;
   Hearts beat and guns leap higher.
Through bloody gaps the boarders swarm,
But still our English stay the storm,
The bulwark in their breast is firm.

Ship after ship, like broken waves
   That wash up on a rock,
Those mighty galleons fall back foiled,
   And shattered from the shock.
With fire she answers all their blows;
Again, again in pieces strows
The burning girdle of her foes.

Through all the night the great white storm
   Of worlds in silence rolled;
Sirius with his sapphire sparkle,
   Mars in ruddy gold.
Heaven looked with stillness terrible
Down on a fight most fierce and fell, —
A sea transfigured into hell.

Some know not of their wounds until
   'T is slippery where they stand:
Then each one tighter grips his steel,
   As 't were salvation's hand.
Wild faces glow through lurid night
With sweat of spirit shining bright:
Only the dead on deck turn white.

At daybreak the flame-picture fades,
　In blackness and in blood;
There, after fifteen hours of fight,
　The unconquered Sea King stood,
Defying all the power of Spain :
Fifteen Armadas hurled in vain,
And fifteen hundred foeman slain.

Around that little bark Revenge
　The baffled Spaniards ride
At distance.　Two of their good ships
　Were sunken at her side;
The rest lie round her in a ring,
As round the dying lion king
The dogs, afraid of his death-spring.

Our pikes all broken, powder spent,
　Sails, masts to shreds were blown;
And with her dead and wounded crew
　The ship was going down!
Sir Richard's wounds were hot and deep.
Then cried he, with a proud, pale lip,
' Ho, gunner, split and sink the ship!

' Make ready now, my mariners,
　To go aloft with me,
That nothing to the Spaniard
　May remain of victory.
They cannot take us, nor we yield;
So let us leave our battle-field
Under the shelter of God's shield.'

They had not heart to dare fulfil
   The stern commander's word:
With bloody hands and weeping eyes
   They carried him aboard
The Spaniards' ship; and round him stand
The warriors of his wasted band:
Then said he, feeling death at hand,

'Here die I, Richard Grenville,
   With a joyful and quiet mind;
I reach a soldier's end, I leave
   A soldier's fame behind,
Who for his queen and country fought,
For honor and religion wrought,
And died as a true soldier ought.'

Earth never returned a worthier trust
   For hand of Heaven to take,
Since Arthur's sword Excalibur
   Was cast into the lake,
And the king's grievous wounds were dressed
And healed by weeping queens, who blessed,
And bore him to a valley of rest.

Old heroes who could grandly do,
   As they could greatly dare, —
A vesture very glorious
   Their shining spirits wear,
Of noble deeds. God give us grace,
That we may see such face to face,
In our great day that comes apace.

By Elizabeth Barrett Browning.

THE FORCED RECRUIT.

SOLFERINO, 1859.

In the ranks of the Austrian you found him,
  He died with his face to you all ;
Yet bury him here where around him
  You honor your bravest that fall.

Venetian, fair-featured and slender,
  He lies shot to death in his youth,
With a smile on his lips over-tender
  For any mere soldier's dead mouth.

No stranger, and yet not a traitor,
  Though alien the cloth on his breast ;
Underneath it how seldom a greater
  Young heart has a shot sent to rest !

By your enemy tortured and goaded
  To march with them, stand in their file,
His musket (see) never was loaded,
  He facing your guns with that smile !

As orphans yearn on to their mothers,
  He yearned to your patriot bands, —
' Let me die for our Italy, brothers,
  If not in your ranks, by your hands !

' Aim straightly, fire steadily ! spare me
    A ball in the body which may
Deliver my heart here, and tear me
    This badge of the Austrian away !'

So thought he, so died he this morning.
    What then ? many others have died.
Ay, but easy for men to die scorning
    The death-stroke, who fought side by side, —

One tricolor floating above them ;
    Struck down mid triumphant acclaims
Of an Italy rescued to love them,
    And brazen the brass with their names.

But he, without witness or honor,
    Mixed, shamed in his country's regard,
With the tyrants who march in upon her,
    Died faithful and passive : 't was hard.

'Twas sublime.   In a cruel restriction
    Cut off from the guerdon of sons,
With most filial obedience, conviction,
    His soul kissed the lips of her guns.

That moves you ?   Nay, grudge not to show it,
    While digging a grave for him here :
The others who died, says your poet,
    Have glory, — let *him* have a tear.

By William Barnes.

THE LOVE-CHILD.

WHERE the bridge out at Woodley did stride,
  Wi' his wide arches' cool sheäded bow,
Up above the clear brook that did slide
  By the popples, befoamed white as snow:
As the gilcups did quiver among
  The white deäisies, a-spread in a sheet,
There a quick-trippèn maïd come along, —
  Aye, a girl wi' her light-steppèn veet.

An' she cried, ' I do praÿ, is the road
  Out to Lincham on here, by the meäd ? '
An' ' Oh, ees,' I meäde answer, an' showed
  Her the way it would turn an' would leäd :
' Goo along by the beech in the nook,
  Where the childern do plaÿ in the cool,
To the steppèn stwones over the brook, —
  Aye, the gray blocks o' rock at the pool.

' Then you don't seem a-born an' a-bred,'
  I spoke up, ' at a place here about ; '
An' she answered wi' cheäks up so red
  As a pi'ny but leäte a-come out :
' No, I lived wi' my uncle that died
  Back in Eäpril, an' now I 'm a·come
Here to Ham, to my mother, to bide, —
  Aye, to her house to vind a new hwome ; '

I 'm asheämed that I wanted to know
    Any mwore of her childhood or life,
But then, why should so feäir a child grow
    Where noo father did bide wi' his wife?
Then wi' blushes of zunrisèn morn,
    She replied, 'That it midden be known,
Oh, they zent me awaÿ to be born, —
    Aye, they hid me when zome would be shown!'

Oh, it meäde me a'most teary-eyed,
    An' I vound I a'most could ha' groaned;
What! so winnèn, an' still cast a-zide, —
    What! so lovely, an' not to be owned!
Oh, a God-gift a-treated wi' scorn;
    Oh, a child that a squier should own;
An' to zend her awaÿ to be born, —
    Aye, to hide her where others be shown!

By James Russell Lowell.

THE COURTIN'.

GOD makes sech nights, all white an' still
    Fur 'z you can look or listen,
Moonshine an' snow on field an' hill,
    All silence an' all glisten.

Zekle crep' up, quite unbeknown,
    An' peeked in thru the winder,
An' there sot Huldy all alone,
    'Ith no one nigh to hender.

A fireplace filled the room's one side
    With half a cord o' wood in —
There warnt no stoves (tell comfort died)
    To bake ye to a puddin'.

The wa'nut logs shot sparkles out
    Towards the pootiest, bless her!
An' leetle flames danced all about
    The chiny on the dresser.

Agin the chimbley crooknecks hung,
    An' in amongst 'em rusted
The ole queen's-arm thet gran'ther Young
    Fetched back from Concord busted.

2

The very room, coz she was in,
    Seemed warm from floor to ceilin',
An' she looked full ez rosy agin
    Ez the apples she was peelin'.

'T was kin' o' kingdom-come to look
    On sech a blessed cretur;
A dogrose blushin' to a brook
    Ain't modester nor sweeter.

He was six foot o' man, A 1,
    Clean grit an' human natur';
None could n't quicker pitch a ton
    Nor dror a furrer straighter.

He 'd sparked it with full twenty gals,
    Hed squired 'em, danced 'em, druv 'em,
Fust this one, an' then thet, by spells —
    All is, he could n't love 'em.

But long o' her his veins 'ould run
    All crinkly like curled maple;
The side she breshed felt full o' sun
    Ez a south slope in Ap'il.

She thought no v'ice hed sech a swing
    Ez hisn in the choir;
My! when he made Ole Hunderd ring,
    She *knowed* the Lord was nigher.

An' she 'd blush scarlit, right in prayer,
    When her new meetin'-bunnet
Felt somehow thru its crown a pair
    O' blue eyes sot upon it.

Thet night, I tell ye, she looked *some!*
   She seemed to 've gut a new soul,
For she felt sartin-sure he 'd come,
   Down to her very shoe-sole.

She heered a foot, an' knowed it tu,
   A-raspin' on the scraper, —
All ways to once her feelin's flew,
   Like sparks in burnt-up paper.

He kin' o' l'itered on the mat,
   Some doubtfle o' the sekle ;
His heart kep' goin' pity-pat,
   But hern went pity Zekle.

An' yit she gin her cheer a jerk
   Ez though she wished him furder,
An' on her apples kep' to work,
   Parin' away like murder.

' You want to see my Pa, I s'pose ? '
   ' Wal, no ; I come dasignin' —'
' To see my Ma?   She 's sprinklin' clo'es
   Agin to-morrer's i'nin'.'

To say why gals act so or so,
   Or don't, 'ould be presumin';
Mebby to mean *yes* an' say *no*
   Comes nateral to women.

He stood a spell on one foot fust,
   Then stood a spell on t' other,
An' on which one he felt the wust
   He could n't ha' told ye nuther.

Says he, ' I 'd better call agin ; '
   Says she, ' Think likely, Mister : '
That last word pricked him like a pin,
   An' — wal, he up an' kist her.

When Ma bimeby upon 'em slips,
   Huldy sot pale ez ashes,
All kin' o' smily roun' the lips
   An' teary roun' the lashes.

For she was jes' the quiet kind
   Whose naturs never vary,
Like streams that keep a summer mind
   Snowhid in Jenooary.

The blood clost roun' her heart felt glued
   Too tight for all expressin',
Tell mother see how metters stood,
   And gin 'em both her blessin'.

Then her red come back like the tide
   Down to the Bay o' Fundy,
An' all I know is they was cried
   In meetin', come nex' Sunday.

By Sir Samuel Fergusson.

WILLY GILLILAND.

AN ULSTER BALLAD.

UP in the mountain solitudes, and in a rebel ring,
He has worshipped God upon the hill, in spite of church
    and king;
And sealed his treason with his blood on Bothwell bridge
    he hath,
So he must fly his father's land, or he must die the death;
For comely Claverhouse has come along with grim Dalzell,
And his smoking roof-tree testifies they've done their
    errand well.

In vain to fly his enemies he fled his native land,
Hot persecution waited him upon the Carrick strand;
His name was on the Carrick cross, a price was on his head,
A fortune to the man that brings him in alive or dead!
And so on moor and mountain, from the Lagan to the Bann,
From house to house, and hill to hill, he lurked an out-
    lawed man.

At last, when in false company he might no longer bide,
He staid his houseless wanderings upon the Collon side,
There in a cave all under ground he laired his heathy den,
Ah, many a gentleman was fain to earth like hill fox then!

With hound and fishing-rod he lived on hill and stream by
    day;
At night, betwixt his fleet greyhound and his bonny mare
    he lay.

It was a summer evening, and, mellowing and still,
Glenwhirry to the setting sun lay bare from hill to hill;
For all that valley pastoral held neither house nor tree,
But spread abroad and open all, a full fair sight to see,
From Slemish foot to Collon top lay one unbroken green,
Save where in many a silver coil the river glanced between.

And on the river's grassy bank, even from the morning gray,
He at the angler's pleasant sport had spent the summer day:
Ah! many a time and oft I 've spent the summer day from
    dawn,
And wondered, when the sunset came, where time and care
    had gone,
Along the reaches curling fresh, the wimpling pools and
    streams,
Where he that day his cares forgot in those delightful
    dreams.

His blithe work done, upon a bank the outlaw rested now,
And laid the basket from his back, the bonnet from his
    brow;
And there, his hand upon the Book, his knee upon the sod,
He filled the lonely valley with the gladsome word of God;
And for a persecuted kirk, and for her martyrs dear,
And against a godless church and king he spoke up loud
    and clear.

And now, upon his homeward way, he crossed the Collon
    high,
And over bush and bank and brae he sent abroad his eye;
But all was darkening peacefully in gray and purple haze,
The thrush was silent in the banks, the lark upon the
    braes;
When suddenly shot up a blaze,—from the cave's mouth it
    came;
And troopers' steeds and troopers' caps are glancing in the
    same !

He couched among the heather, and he saw them, as he
    lay,
With three long yells at parting, ride lightly east away:
Then down with heavy heart he came, to sorry cheer
    came he,
For ashes black were crackling where the green whins
    used to be,
And stretched among the prickly coomb, his heart's blood
    smoking round,
From slender nose to breastbone cleft, lay dead his good
    greyhound !

'They've slain my dog, the Philistines! they've ta'en my
    bonny mare !'
He plunged into the smoky hole, — no bonny beast was
    there;
He groped beneath his burning bed (it burned him to the
    bone),
Where his good weapon used to be, but broadsword there
    was none;

He reeled out of the stifling den, and sat down on a stone,
And in the shadows of the night 't was thus he made his
      moan : —

' I am a houseless outcast ; I have neither bed nor board.
Nor living thing to look upon, nor comfort, save the Lord :
Yet many a time were better men in worse extremity ;
Who succored them in their distress, He now will succor
      me, —
He now will succor me, I know ; and, by His holy Name,
I 'll make the doers of this deed right dearly rue the same !

' My bonny mare ! I 've ridden you when Claver'se rode
      behind,
And from the thumbscrew and the boot you bore me like
      the wind :
And while I have the life you saved, on your sleek flank,
      I swear,
Episcopalian rowel shall never ruffle hair !
Though sword to wield they 've left me none, yet Wallace
      wight, I wis,
Good battle did on Irvine side wi' waur weapon than this.'

His fishing-rod with both his hands he griped it as he spoke,
And where the butt and top were spliced, in pieces twain
      he broke ;
The limber top he cast away, with all its gear abroad,
But, grasping the tough hickory butt, with spike of iron
      shod,
He ground the sharp spear to a point ; then pulled his
      bonnet down,
And, meditating black revenge, set forth for Carrick town.

The sun shines bright on Carrick wall and Carrick Castle
     gray,
And up thine aisle, Saint Nicholas, has ta'en his morning
     way ;
And to the North-Gate sentinel displayeth far and near
Sea, hill, and tower, and all thereon, in dewy freshness
     clear,
Save where, behind a ruined wall, himself alone to view,
Is peering from the ivy green a bonnet of the blue.

The sun shines red on Carrick wall and Carrick castle old,
And all the western buttresses have changed their gray for
     gold ;
And from thy shrine, Saint Nicholas, the pilgrim of the sky
Hath gone in rich farewell, as fits such royal votary ;
But as his last red glance he takes down past black Slieve-
     a-true,
He leaveth where he found it first the bonnet of the blue.

Again he makes the turrets gray stand out before the hill ;
Constant as their foundation rock, there is the bonnet still !
And now the gates are opened, and forth in gallant show
Prick jeering grooms and burghers blithe, and troopers in
     a row ;
But one has little care for jest, so hard bested is he,
To ride the outlaw's bonny mare, for this at last is she !

Down comes her master with a roar, her rider with a groan,
The iron and the hickory are through and through him
     gone !
He lies a corpse ; and where he sat, the outlaw sits again,

And once more to his bonny mare he gives the spur and
     rein ;
Then some with sword, and some with gun, they ride and
     run amain ;
But sword and gun, and whip and spur, that day they plied
     in vain !

Ah ! little thought Willy Gilliland, when he on Skerry side
Drew bridle first, and wiped his brow after that weary ride,
That where he lay like hunted brute, a caverned outlaw
     lone,
Broad lands and yeomen tenantry should yet be there his
     own ;
Yet so it was ; and still from him descendants not a few
Draw birth and lands, and, let me trust, draw love of Free-
     dom too.

By George Macdonald.

BALLAD OF THE THULIAN NURSE.

'SWEEP up the flure, Janet;
  Put on anither peat;
It 's a lown and starry nicht, Janet,
  And neither cauld nor weet.

' And it 's open hoose we keep the nicht
  For ony that may be oot.
It 's the nicht atween the Sancts and Souls,
  Whan the bodiless gang aboot.

' Set the chairs back to the wa', Janet;
  Mak' ready for quaiet fowk.
Hae a' thing as clean as a win'in'-sheet:
  They come na ilka ook.

' There 's a spale upo' the flure, Janet,
  And there 's a rowan-berry;
Sweep them into the fire, Janet, —
  They 'll be welcomer than merry.

'Syne set open the door, Janet —
  Wide open for wha kens wha;
As ye come benn to yer bed, Janet,
  Set it open to the wa'.'

She set the chairs back to the wa',
  But ane made o' the birk;
She sweepit the flure, — left that ae spale,
  A lang spale o' the aik.

The nicht was lowne, and the stars sat still,
  Aglintin' doon the sky;
And the souls crap oot o' their mooly graves,
  A' dank wi' lyin' by.

She had set the door wide to the wa',
  And blawn the peats rosy reed;
They war shoonless feet gaed oot and in,
  Nor clampit as they gaed.

Whan midnicht cam', the mither rase —
  She wad gae see and hear.
Back she cam' wi' a glowerin' face,
  And sloomin' wi' verra fear.

'There's ane o' them sittin' afore the fire !
  Janet, gang na to see:
Ye left a chair afore the fire,
  Whaur I tauld ye nae chair sud be.'

Janet she smiled in her mother's face:
  She had brunt the noddin reid;
And she left aneath the birken chair
  The spale frae a coffin-lid.

She rase and she gaed butt the hoose,
    Aye steekin' door and door.
Three hours gaed by or her mother heard
    Her fit upo' the flure.

But whan the grey cock crew, she heard
    The sound o' shoonless feet;
When the red cock crew, she heard the door,
    And a sough o' wind and weet.

And Janet cam' back wi' a wan face,
    But never a word said she;
No man ever heard her voice lood oot,
    It cam' like frae ower the sea.

And no man ever heard her lauch,
    Nor yet say alas or wae;
But a smile aye glimmert on her wan face,
    Like the moonlicht on the sea.

And ilka nicht 'tween the Saints and the Souls,
    Wide open she set the door;
And she mendit the fire, and she left ae chair,
    And that spale upo' the flure.

And at midnicht she gaed butt the hoose,
    Aye steekin' door and door;
Whan the reid cock crew, she cam' benn the hoose,
    Aye wanner than afore —

Wanner her face, and sweeter her smile;
    Till the seventh All Souls' eve.
Her mother she heard the shoonless feet,
    Said, 'She 's comin', I believe.'

But she camna benn, and her mother lay ;
  For fear she cudna stan'.
But up she rase and benn she gaed,
  Whan the gowden cock had crawn.

And Janet sat upo' the chair,
  White as the day did daw ;
Her smile was the sunlicht left on the sea,
  Whan the sun has gone awa'.

By Sir Francis Hastings Charles Doyle.

THE DONCASTER ST. LEGER.[1]

THE sun is bright, the sky is clear,
  Above the crowded course,
As the mighty moment draweth near
  Whose issue shows *the horse.*

The fairest of the land are here
To watch the struggle of the year ;
The dew of beauty and of mirth
Lies on the living flowers of earth,
And blushing cheek and kindling eye
Lend brightness to the sun on high ;
And every corner of the north
Has poured her hardy yeoman forth :
The dweller by the glistening rills
That sound among the Craven hills ;
The stalwart husbandman who holds
His plough upon the eastern wolds ;
The sallow shrivelled artisan,
Twisted below the height of man,
Whose limbs and life have mouldered down
Within some foul and cloudy town,

Are gathered thickly on the lea,
Or streaming from far homes to see
If Yorkshire keeps her old renown;
Or if the dreaded Derby horse
Can sweep in triumph o'er her course.
With the same look in every face,
The same keen feeling, they retrace
The legends of each ancient race :
Recalling Reveller in his pride,
Or Blacklock of the mighty stride,
Or listening to some gray-haired sage
Full of the dignity of age, —
How Hambletonian beat of yore
Such rivals as are seen no more ;
How his old father loved to tell
Of that long struggle — ended well —
When, strong of heart, the Wentworth Bay
From staggering Herod strode away;
How Yorkshire racers, swift as they,
Would leave this southern horse half-way ;
But that the creatures of to-day
Are cast in quite a different mould
From what he recollects of old.
Clear peals the bell; at that known sound,
Like bees, the people cluster round ;
On either side upstarting then,
One close dark wall of breathless men,
Far down as eye can stretch, is seen
Along yon vivid strip of green,
Where, keenly watched by countless eyes,
'Mid hopes, and fears, and prophecies,

Now fast, now slow, now here, now there,
With hearts of fire and limbs of air,
Snorting and prancing, — sidling by
With arching neck and glancing eye,
In every shape of strength and grace
The horses gather for the race;
Soothed for a moment all, they stand
Together, like a sculptured band;
Each quivering eyelid flutters thick,
Each face is flushed, each heart beats quick;
And all around dim murmurs pass
Like low winds moaning on the grass.
Again, the thrilling signal sound;
And off at once, with one long bound,
Into the speed of thought they leap,
Like a proud ship rushing to the deep.
A start! a start! they 're off, by Heaven!
Like a single horse, though twenty-seven,
And mid the flash of silks we scan
A Yorkshire Jacket in the van;
    Hurrah! for the bold bay mare!

I 'll pawn my soul her place is there
    Unheaded to the last,
For a thousand pounds, she wins unpast —
    Hurrah! for the matchless mare!

A hundred yards have glided by,
    And they settle to the race;
More keen becomes each straining eye,
    More terrible the pace.

Unbroken yet o'er the gravel road
Like maddening waves the troop has flowed,
    But the speed begins to tell;
And Yorkshire sees, with eye of fear,
The Southron stealing from the rear.
    Ay! mark his action well!
Behind he is, but what repose!
How steadily and clean he goes!
What latent speed his limbs disclose!
What power in every stride he shows!
They see, they feel; from man to man
The shivering thrill of terror ran,
And every soul instinctive knew
It lay between the mighty two.
The world without, the sky above,
    Have glided from their straining eyes, —
Future and past, and hate and love,
    The life that wanes, the friend that dies.
E'en grim remorse, who sits behind
Each thought and motion of the mind,
These now are nothing, Time and Space
Lie in the rushing of the race,
As with keen shouts of hope and fear
They watch it in its wild career.
Still far ahead of the glittering throng
Dashes the eager mare along,
And round the turn, and past the hill,
Slides up the Derby winner still.
The twenty-five that lay between
Are blotted from the stirring scene,
And the wild cries which rang so loud,

Sink by degrees throughout the crowd,
To one deep humming, like the tremulous roar
Of seas remote along a northern shore.

In distance dwindling to the eye
Right opposite the stand they lie,
And scarcely seem to stir;
Though an Arab scheich his wives would give
For a single steed, that with them could live
Three hundred yards, without the spur.
But though so indistinct and small
You hardly see them move at all,
There are not wanting signs which show
Defeat is busy as they go.
Look how the mass, which rushed away
As full of spirit as the day,
So close compacted for a while,
Is lengthening into single file.
Now inch by inch it breaks, and wide
And spreading gaps the line divide.
As forward still, and far away
Undulates on the tired array,
Gay colors, momently less bright,
Fade flickering on the gazers' sight,
Till keenest eyes can scarcely trace
The homeward ripple of the race.
Care sits on every lip and brow:
' Who leads? who fails? how goes it now?'
One shooting spark of life intense,
One throb of refluent suspense,
And a far rainbow-colored light

Trembles again upon the sight.
Look to yon turn!   Already there
Gleams the pink and black of the fiery mare,
And through *that* which was but now a gap,
Creeps on the terrible white cap.
Half-strangled in each throat, a shout,
Wrung from their fevered spirits out,
Booms through the crowd like muffled drums,
'His jockey moves on him.   He comes!'
Then momently, like gusts, you heard,
'He 's sixth — he 's fifth — he 's fourth — he 's third!'
And on, like some glancing meteor-flame,
The stride of the Derby winner came.

And during all that anxious time
(Sneer as it suits you at my rhyme)
The earnestness became sublime;
Common and trite as is the scene,
At once so thrilling and so mean,
To him who strives his heart to scan,
And feels the brotherhood of man,
That needs *must* be a mighty minute,
When a crowd has but one soul within it.
As some bright ship, with every sail
Obedient to the urging gale,
Darts by vext hulls, which side by side,
Dismasted on the raging tide,
Are struggling onward, wild and wide,
Thus through the reeling field he flew,
And near and yet more near he drew;
Each leap seems longer than the last,

Now   now — the second horse is past,
And the keen rider of the mare,
With haggard looks of feverish care,
Hangs forward on the speechless air,
By steady stillness nursing in
The remnant of her speed to win.
One other bound — one more — 't is done;
Right up to her the horse has run,
And head to head, and stride for stride,
Newmarket's hope and Yorkshire's pride,
Like horses harnessed side by side,
    Are struggling to the goal.
Ride! gallant son of Ebor, ride!
For the dear honor of the north
Stretch every bursting sinew forth,
    Put out thy inmost soul, —
And with knee, and thigh, and tightened rein
Lift in the mare by might and main;
The feelings of the people reach,
What lies beyond the springs of speech,
So that there rises up no sound
From the wide human life around;
One spirit flashes from each eye,
One impulse lifts each heart throat-high,
One short and panting silence broods
O'er the wildly-working multitudes,
As on the struggling coursers press,
So deep the eager silentness,
That underneath their feet the turf
Seems shaken, like the eddying surf
    When it tastes the rushing gale,

And the singing fall of the heavy whips,
Which tear the flesh away in strips,
    As the tempest tears the sail,
On the throbbing heart and quivering ear
Strike vividly distinct and near.
But mark what an arrowy rush is there,
'He 's beat ! he 's beat ! ' — by Heaven, the mare !
Just on the post, her spirit rare,
When Hope herself might well despair ;
When time had not a breath to spare ;
With birdlike dash shoots clean away,
And by half a length has gained the day.
Then how to life that silence wakes !
Ten thousand hats thrown up on high
Send darkness to the echoing sky,
And like the crash of hill-pent lakes,
Outbursting from their deepest fountains,
Among the rent and reeling mountains,
At once, from thirty thousand throats
    Rushes the Yorkshire roar,
And the name of their northern winner floats
    A league from the course, and more.

By *Jean Ingelow*

WINSTANLEY.[2]

THE APOLOGY.

Quoth the cedar to the reeds and rushes,
  ' Water-grass, you know not what I do ;
Know not of my storms, nor of my hushes,
  And — I know not you.'

Quoth the reeds and rushes, ' Wind ! oh, waken !
  Breathe, O wind, and set our answer free ;
For we have no voice, of you forsaken,
  For the cedar-tree.'

Quoth the earth at midnight to the ocean,
  ' Wilderness of water, lost to view,
Naught you are to me but sounds of motion ;
  I am naught to you.'

Quoth the ocean, ' Dawn ! O fairest, clearest,
  Touch me with thy golden fingers bland ;
For I have no smile till thou appearest
  For the lovely land.'

Quoth the hero dying, whelmed in glory,
  ' Many blame me, few have understood ;
Ah, my folk, to you I leave a story, —
  Make its meaning good '

Quoth the folk, ' Sing, poet ! teach us, prove us ;
  Surely we shall learn the meaning then ;
Wound us with a pain divine, oh, move us,
  For this man of men.'

WINSTANLEY'S deed, you kindly folk,
  With it I fill my lay,
And a nobler man ne'er walked the world,
  Let his name be what it may.

The good ship ' Snowdrop ' tarried long,
  Up at the vane looked he ;
' Belike,' he said, for the wind had dropped,
  ' She lieth becalmed at sea.'

The lovely ladies flocked within,
  And still would each one say,
' Good mercer, be the ships come up ? '
  But still he answered, ' Nay.'

Then stepped two mariners down the street,
  With looks of grief and fear,
' Now, if Winstanley be your name,
  We bring you evil cheer !

' For the good ship " Snowdrop " struck, — she struck
  On the rock — the Eddystone,
And down she went with threescore men,
  We two being left alone.

Down in the deep, with freight and crew,
  Past any help she lies,
And never a bale has come to shore
  Of all thy merchandise.'

' For cloth o' gold and comely frieze,'
　　Winstanley said, and sighed,
' For velvet coif, or costly coat,
　　They fathoms deep may bide.

' O thou brave skipper, blithe and kind,
　　O mariners, bold and true,
Sorry at heart, right sorry am I,
　　A-thinking of yours and you.

' Many long days Winstanley's breast
　　Shall feel a weight within,
For a waft of wind he shall be 'feared,
　　And trading count but sin.

' To him no more it shall be joy
　　To pace the cheerful town,
And see the lovely ladies gay
　　Step on in velvet gown.'

The ' Snowdrop' sank at Lammas tide
　　All under the yeasty spray ;
On Christmas Eve the brig ' Content '
　　Was also cast away.

He little thought o' New Year's night,
　　So jolly as he sat then,
While drank the toast and praised the roast
　　The round-faced Aldermen, --

While serving-lads ran to and fro,
　　Pouring the ruby wine,
And jellies trembled on the board,
　　And towering pasties fine, —

While loud huzzas ran up the roof
 Till the lamps did rock o'erhead,
And holly-boughs from rafters hung
 Dropped down their berries red, —

He little thought on Plymouth Hoe,
 With every rising tide,
How the wave washed in his sailor lads,
 And laid them side by side.

There stepped a stranger to the board :
 ' Now, stranger, who be ye ? '
He looked to right, he looked to left,
 And ' Rest you merry,' quoth he ;

' For you did not see the brig go down,
 Or ever a storm had blown ;
For you did not see the white wave rear
 At the rock, — the Eddystone.

' She drave at the rock with sternsails set ;
 Crash went the masts in twain ;
She staggered back with her mortal blow,
 Then leaped at it again.

' There rose a great cry, bitter and strong,
 The misty moon looked out !
And the water swarmed with seamen's heads,
 And the wreck was strewed about.

' I saw her mainsail lash the sea
 As I clung to the rock alone ;
Then she heeled over, and down she went,
 And sank like any stone.

' She was a fair ship, but all 's one !
   For naught could bide the shock.'
' I will take horse,' Winstanley said,
   ' And see this deadly rock ;

' For never again shall bark o' mine
   Sail over the windy sea,
Unless, by the blessing of God, for this
   Be found a remedy.'

Winstanley rode to Plymouth town
   All in the sleet and the snow,
And he looked around on shore and sound
   As he stood on Plymouth Hoe,

Till a pillar of spray rose far away,
   And shot up its stately head,
Reared and fell over, and reared again :
   '' T is the rock ! the rock !' he said.

Straight to the Mayor he took his way,
   ' Good Master Mayor,' quoth he,
' I am a mercer of London town,
   And owner of vessels three, —

' But for your rock of dark renown,
   I had five to track the main.'
' You are one of many,' the old Mayor said,
   ' That on the rock complain.

' An ill rock, mercer ! your words ring right,
   Well with my thoughts they chime,
For my two sons to the world to come
   It sent before their time.'

' Lend me a lighter, good Master Mayor,
    And a score of shipwrights free,
For I think to raise a lantern tower
    On this rock o' destiny.'

The old Mayor laughed, but sighed alsó;
    ' Ah, youth,' quoth he, ' is rash ;
Sooner, young man, thou 'lt root it out
    From the sea that doth it lash.

' Who sails too near its jagged teeth,
    He shall have evil lot :
For the calmest seas that tumble there
    Froth like a boiling pot.

' And the heavier seas few look on nigh,
    But straight they lay him dead :
A seventy-gun-ship, sir, they 'll shoot
    Higher than her mast-head.

' Oh, beacons sighted in the dark,
    They are right welcome things,
And pitchpots flaming on the shore
    Show fair as angel wings.

' Hast gold in hand ? then light the land,
    It 'longs to thee and me ;
But let alone the deadly rock
    In God Almighty's sea.'

Yet said he, ' Nay. — I must away,
    On the rock to set my feet ;
My debts are paid, my will I made,
    Or ever I did thee greet.

'If I must die, then let me die
    By the rock, and not elsewhere;
If I may live, oh, let me live
    To mount my lighthouse stair.'

The old Mayor looked him in the face,
    And answered: 'Have thy way;
Thy heart is stout, as if round about
    It was braced with an iron stay:

'Have thy will, mercer! choose thy men,
    Put off from the storm-rid shore;
God with thee be, or I shall see
    Thy face and theirs no more.'

Heavily plunged the breaking wave,
    And foam flew up the lea,
Morning and even the drifted snow
    Fell into the dark gray sea.

Winstanley chose him men and gear:
    He said, 'My time I waste,'
For the seas ran seething up the shore,
    And the wrack drave on in haste.

But twenty days he waited, and more,
    Pacing the strand alone,
Or ever he set his manly foot
    On the rock, — the Eddystone.

Then he and the sea began their strife,
    And worked with power and might:
Whatever the man reared up by day
    The sea broke down by night.

He wrought at ebb with bar and beam,
    He sailed to shore at flow ;
And at his side, by that same tide,
    Came bar and beam alsó.

' Give in, give in,' the old Mayor criéd,
    ' Or thou wilt rue the day.'
' Yonder he goes,' the townsfolk sighed,
    ' But the rock will have its way.

' For all his looks that are so stout,
    And his speeches brave and fair,
He may wait on the wind, wait on the wave,
    But he 'll build no lighthouse there.'

In fine weather and foul weather
    The rock his arts did flout,
Through the long days and the short days,
    Till all that year ran out.

With fine weather and foul weather
    Another year came in :
' To take his wage,' the workmen said,
    ' We almost count a sin.'

Now March was gone, came April in,
    And a sea-fog settled down,
And forth sailed he on a glassy sea, —
    He sailed from Plymouth town.

With men and stores he put to sea,
    As he was wont to do ;
They showed in the fog like ghosts full faint, —
    A ghostly craft and crew.

And the sea-fog lay and waxed alway,
  For a long eight days and more ;
' God help our men,' quoth the women then ;
  ' For they bide long from shore.'

They paced the Hoe in doubt and dread :
  ' Where may our mariners be ? '
But the brooding fog lay soft as down
  Over the quiet sea.

A Scottish schooner made the port
  The thirteenth day at e'en.
' As I am a man,' the captain cried,
  ' A strange sight I have seen :

' And a strange sound heard, my masters all,
  At sea, in the fog and the rain,
Like shipwrights' hammers tapping low,
  Then loud, then low again.

' And a stately house one instant showed,
  Through a rift, on the vessel's lee ;
What manner of creatures may be those
  That build upon the sea ? '

Then sighed the folk, ' The Lord be praised ! '
  And they flocked to the shore amain ;
All over the Hoe, that livelong night,
  Many stood out in the rain.

It ceased, and the red sun reared his head,
  And the rolling fog did flee ;
And lo ! in the offing faint and far
  Winstanley's house at sea !

In fair weather with mirth and cheer
   The stately tower uprose;
In foul weather, with hunger and cold,
   They were content to close;

Till up the stair Winstanley went,
   To fire the wick afar;
And Plymouth in the silent night
   Looked out, and saw her star.

Winstanley set his foot ashore:
   Said he, ' My work is done;
I hold it strong to last as long
   As aught beneath the sun.

' But if it fail, as fail it may,
   Borne down with ruin and rout,
Another than I shall rear it high,
   And brace the girders stout.

' A better than I shall rear it high,
   For now the way is plain ;
And though I were dead,' Winstanley said,
   ' The light would shine again.

' Yet, were I fain still to remain,
   Watch in my tower to keep,
And tend my light in the stormiest night
   That ever did move the deep;

' And if it stood, why, then 't were good,
   Amid their tremulous stirs,
To count each stroke, when the mad waves broke,
   For cheers of mariners.

'But if it fell, then this were well,
    That I should with it fall;
Since, for my part, I have built my heart
    In the courses of its wall.

'Ay! I were fain long to remain,
    Watch in my tower to keep,
And tend my light in the stormiest night
    That ever did move the deep.'

With that Winstanley went his way,
    And left the rock renowned,
And summer and winter his pilot star
    Hung bright o'er Plymouth Sound.

But it fell out, fell out at last,
    That he would put to sea,
To scan once more his lighthouse tower
    On the rock o' destiny.

And the winds broke, and the storm broke,
    And wrecks came plunging in;
None in the town that night lay down
    Or sleep or rest to win.

The great mad waves were rolling graves,
    And each flung up its dead;
The seething flow was white below,
    And black the sky o'erhead.

And when the dawn, the dull, gray dawn,
    Broke on the trembling town,
And men looked south to the harbor mouth,
    The lighthouse tower was down, —

Down in the deep where he doth sleep
  Who made it shine afar,
And then in the night that drowned its light
  Set, with his pilot star.

Many fair tombs in the glorious glooms
  At Westminster they show;
The brave and the great lie there in state:
  Winstanley lieth low.

By Sabine Baring-Gould.

THE MASS FOR THE DEAD.[a]

A LEGEND OF MESSINA.

ALL day unflagging in his stall
   Sat Hildebrand the priest, and heard
Confessions made, and over all
   He uttered the absolving word.

But as the light of garish day
Passed with the setting sun away,
A heaviness and languor stole
All unperceived upon his soul.

Full oft at the confided sin
   The tender-hearted priest had wept;
Now wearied, as the dusk set in,
   He leaned him back and slept.

Nor woke he to the vesper bell,
Nor heard the organ's solemn swell,
And only turned upon his seat
At tramp of the retreating feet.

Heard not the verger's closing call,
   Nor chiming of the transept clock,
Heard not the doors together fall,
   Nor noisy key turned in the lock.

And as the night hours glided by,
And Charles's Wain wheeled in the sky,
Priest Hildebrand slept heavily.

Now first a spark, and then a flame,
Like an uplighted beacon, came ;
And next a streak of silver light
That smote along the vaulted height,
As above the eastern deep
Slow the moon's white horn did peep.

Sudden pealed the watchman's blast
When the noon of night was past,
And the echoes clung awhile
To the ribbing of the aisle.
Still did the slumb'ring pastor rest
With gray head nodding on his breast.

And thus the night hours glided by,
As Charles's Wain wheeled in the sky,
And Hildebrand slept heavily.

The presses and misereres of oak
Warped and snapped : each noisy stroke
Of the minster clock, though clear,
Unheeded fell upon the ear.
A sea-breeze rose, and idly strayed
Over the window glass, and played

Faint pipings where it found a rent,
Or sung about the battlement.

A click — a rush of whirring wheels,
The hammer of the old clock reels,
And strikes one stroke upon the gong,
With long-drawn after undersong.

Then, suddenly, the sleep-bands broke,
And Hildebrand the priest awoke,
And conscious instantly, he gave
One stride, and found him in the nave.
Then started, with a sense of awe,
As he the whole interior saw
With light illumed, but wan and faint,
By which each shrine and sculptured saint,
Each marble shaft and fretted niche,
The moulded arch, the tracery rich,
The brazen eagle in the choir,
The bishop's throne with gilded spire,
Stood out as clear as on a day
When clouds obscure the solar ray.
The altar tapers were alight,
Chalice and paten glimmered bright,
The service-book was opened wide,
Wafers and cruets were at one side.
And on the rail, in meet array,
Alb, amice, stole, and vestment lay.
And one knelt on the altar stair
As server, hushed, immersed in prayer,
In convent garb, and with feet bare.

Now with a shrinking and surprise,
And scarcely crediting his eyes,
The priest discerned the whitened bone
Of feet, where skin and flesh were none.
With quivering knees, and throbbing blood,
And chattering teeth, the roused man stood;
Whilst each vibration of the clock
Beat on his pulse with liveliest shock.

Up rose the monk   and his bones ground
As he arose — and turned him round,
And spread abroad his wasted hands,
As doth the celebrant who stands,
And makes the dread adorèd sign,
To close the mysteries divine.

Sudden a voice the silence broke
With words articulate, and spoke
    From underneath the drooping cowl.
As clear as ring of sanctus bell
Hildebrand heard each syllable:
    'Who mass will offer for my soul?'

'I will!' cried Hildebrand, and strode
Towards the altar of his God.

And so that night it came to pass
A priest intoned the holy mass,
In that cathedral, for one dead,
Whose soul unshriven sufferèd;
And all the while he prayed, he felt
That a dead man behind him knelt.

But on the face he dared not look
Of him who served the holy book,
The cruets, and the sacred bread,
With serge cowl covering his head.

Now, when his office was complete,
He marked the monk upon his knees,
Who muttered, as winds sound in trees,
And, with dead hands, held fast his feet,
Who said:
    'What years of bitter pain
My soul in Purgatory hath lain,
And panted for release in vain!
Beneath yon slab my body lies,
No loving fingers closed my eyes,
But, wrestling in death's agonies,
Alone I breathed my parting sighs.
Yonder was an unguarded well,
Down which, by fatal chance, I fell;
And where I was no mortal knew,
For no man thence the water drew;
And through the town the rumor spread
That from my cloister I had fled.
Thus for my soul no mass was said,
Nor was my body buried.
And, as the well was used no more,
As time passed, it was covered o'er.
But nightly for two hundred years
Here have I cried aloud with tears,
And none have heard my wail till now,
Or answered to my prayer, but thou.

Priest Hildebrand! God's blessing light
Upon thee for thy deed this night.
I would repay, but power have none —
Save this, that ere thy sands are run
    I will appear again.'

And as he spake, a pallid ray,
The harbinger of coming day,
    Smote through the eastern pane.
Then first, enabled by God's grace,
The priest looked on the dead man's face.
That turned towards the Crucified
As in a rapture, glorified.
And with great reverence, Hildebrand,
Extending o'er the monk his hand,
Traced upon the ashy brow
    And the uplifted head
The sacred sign which angels know
And devils fear.   So, saying 'Peace!'
The monk responded, ' With release,'
    And vanishèd.

By Edmund Clarence Stedman.

THE DOORSTEP.

THE conference-meeting through at last,
   We boys around the vestry waited
To see the girls come tripping past
   Like snow-birds willing to be mated.

Not braver he that leaps the wall
   By level musket-flashes litten,
Than I, that stepped before them all
   Who longed to see me get the mitten.

But no, she blushed and took my arm!
   We let the old folks have the highway,
And started toward the Maple Farm
   Along a kind of lovers' by-way.

I can't remember what we said,
   'T was nothing worth a song or story;
Yet that rude path by which we sped
   Seemed all transformed and in a glory.

The snow was crisp beneath our feet,
   The moon was full, the fields were gleaming;
By hood and tippet sheltered sweet,
   Her face with youth and health was beaming.

The little hand outside her muff, —
　O sculptor, if you could but mould it! —
So lightly touched my jacket-cuff,
　To keep it warm I had to hold it.

To have her with me there alone, —
　'T was love and fear and triumph blended.
At last we reached the foot-worn stone
　Where that delicious journey ended.

The old folks, too, were almost home;
　Her dimpled hand the latches fingered,
We heard the voices nearer come,
　Yet on the doorstep still we lingered.

She shook her ringlets from her hood,
　And with a 'Thank you, Ned,' dissembled,
But yet I knew she understood
　With what a daring wish I trembled.

A cloud passed kindly overhead,
　The moon was slyly peeping through it,
Yet hid its face, as if it said,
　'Come, now or never! do it! *do it!* '

My lips till then had only known
　The kiss of mother and of sister;
But somehow, full upon her own
　Sweet, rosy, darling mouth, — I kissed her!

Perhaps 't was boyish love, yet still,
　O listless woman, weary lover!
To feel once more that fresh, wild thrill
　I 'd give — but who can live youth over?

By Christina Georgina Rossetti.

JESSIE CAMERON.

'JESSIE, Jessie Cameron,
  Hear me but this once,' quoth he.
'Good luck go with you, neighbor's son,
  But I'm no mate for you,' quoth she.
Day was verging toward the night
  There beside the moaning sea;
Dimness overtook the light
  There where the breakers be.
'O Jessie, Jessie Cameron,
  I have loved you long and true.' —
'Good luck go with you, neighbor's son,
  But I'm no mate for you.'

She was a careless, fearless girl,
  And made her answer plain;
Outspoken she to earl or churl,
  Kind-hearted in the main,
But somewhat heedless with her tongue,
  And apt at causing pain;
A mirthful maiden she, and young,
  Most fair for bliss or bane.
'Oh, long ago I told you so,
  I tell you so to-day:
Go you your way, and let me go
  Just my own free way.'

The sea swept in with moan and foam
   Quickening the stretch of sand:
They stood almost in sight of home;
   He strove to take her hand.
'Oh, can't you take your answer then,
   And won't you understand?
For me you 're not the man of men,
   I 've other plans are planned.
You 're good for Madge, or good for Cis,
   Or good for Kate, may be:
But what 's to me the good of this,
   While you 're not good for me?'

They stood together on the beach,
   They two alone,
And louder waxed his urgent speech,
   His patience almost gone:
'Oh, say but one kind word to me,
   Jessie, Jessie Cameron.' —
'I 'd be too proud to beg,' quoth she,
   And pride was in her tone.
And pride was in her lifted head, .
   And in her angry eye,
And in her foot, which might have fled,
   But would not fly.

Some say that he had gypsy blood,
   That in his heart was guile:
Yet he had gone through fire and flood
   Only to win her smile.
Some say his grandam was a witch,
   A black witch from beyond the Nile.

Who kept an image in a niche
  And talked with it the while.
And by her hut far down the lane
  Some say they would not pass at night,
Lest they should hear an unked strain
  Or see an unked sight.

Alas, for Jessie Cameron!
  The sea crept moaning, moaning nigher:
She should have hastened to be gone, —
  The sea swept higher, breaking by her:
She should have hastened to her home
  While yet the west was flushed with fire,
But now her feet are in the foam,
  The sea-foam, sweeping higher.
O mother, linger at your door,
  And light your lamp to make it plain;
But Jessie she comes home no more,
  No more again.

They stood together on the strand,
  They only, each by each;
Home, her home, was close at hand,
  Utterly out of reach.
Her mother in the chimney nook
  Heard a startled sea-gull screech,
But never turned her head to look
  Towards the darkening beach:
Neighbors here and neighbors there
  Heard one scream, as if a bird
Shrilly screaming cleft the air, —
  That was all they heard.

Jessie she comes home no more,
    Comes home never;
Her lover's step sounds at his door
    No more forever.
And boats may search upon the sea,
    And search along the river,
But none know where the bodies be:
    Sea-winds that shiver,
Sea-birds that breast the blast,
    Sea-waves swelling,
Keep the secret first and last
    Of their dwelling.

Whether the tide so hemmed them round
    With its pitiless flow,
That when they would have gone they found
    No way to go;
Whether she scorned him to the last
    With words flung to and fro,
Or clung to him when hope was past,
    None will ever know:
Whether he helped or hindered her,
    Threw up his life or lost it well,
The troubled sea, for all its stir,
    Finds no voice to tell.

Only watchers by the dying
    Have thought they heard one pray,
Wordless, urgent; and replying,
    One seem to say him nay:
And watchers by the dead have heard
    A windy swell from miles away,

With sobs and screams, but not a word
   Distinct for them to say:
And watchers out at sea have caught
   Glimpse of a pale gleam here or there,
Come and gone as quick as thought,
   Which might be hand or hair.

By John Hay.

A WOMAN'S LOVE.[8]

A SENTINEL angel sitting high in glory
Heard this shrill wail ring out from Purgatory:
'Have mercy, mighty angel, hear my story!

'I loved,—and, blind with passionate love, I fell.
Love brought me down to death, and death to Hell.
For God is just, and death for sin is well.

'I do not rage against his high decree,
Nor for myself do ask that grace shall be;
But for my love on earth who mourns for me.

'Great Spirit! Let me see my love again
And comfort him one hour, and I were fain
To pay a thousand years of fire and pain.'

Then said the pitying angel, 'Nay, repent
That wild vow! Look, the dial finger 's bent
Down to the last hour of thy punishment!'

But still she wailed, 'I pray thee, let me go!
I cannot rise to peace and leave him so.
Oh, let me soothe him in his bitter woe!'

The brazen gates ground sullenly ajar,
And upward, joyous, like a rising star,
She rose and vanished in the ether far.

But soon adown the dying sunset sailing,
And like a wounded bird her pinions trailing,
She fluttered back, with broken-hearted wailing.

She sobbed, ' I found him by the summer sea
Reclined, his head upon a maiden's knee, —
She curled his hair and kissed him.   Woe is me!'

She wept, ' Now let my punishment begin !
I have been fond and foolish.   Let me in
To expiate my sorrow and my sin.'

The angel answered, ' Nay, sad soul, go higher !
To be deceived in your true heart's desire
Was bitterer than a thousand years of fire!'

By John Greenleaf Whittier.

IN SCHOOL–DAYS.

STILL sits the school-house by the road,
    A ragged beggar sunning;
Around it still the sumachs grow,
    And blackberry vines are running.

Within, the master's desk is seen,
    Deep scarred by raps official;
The warping floor, the battered seats,
    The jack-knife's carved initial;

The charcoal frescos on its wall;
    Its door's worn sill, betraying
The feet that, creeping slow to school,
    Went storming out to playing!

Long years ago a winter sun
    Shone over it at setting;
Lit up its western window-panes,
    And low eaves' icy fretting.

It touched the tangled golden curls,
    And brown eyes full of grieving,
Of one who still her steps delayed
    When all the school were leaving.

For near her stood the little boy
  Her childish favor singled;
His cap pulled low upon a face
  Where pride and shame were mingled.

Pushing with restless feet the snow
  To right and left, he lingered;
As restlessly her tiny hands
  The blue-checked apron fingered.

He saw her lift her eyes; he felt
  The soft hand's light caressing,
And heard the tremble of her voice,
  As if a fault confessing.

' I 'm sorry that I spelt the word:
  I hate to go above you,
Because,' — the brown eyes lower fell, —
  ' Because, you see, I love you!'

Still memory to a gray-haired man
  That sweet child-face is showing.
Dear girl! the grasses on her grave
  Have forty years been growing!

He lives to learn, in life's hard school,
  How few who pass above him
Lament their triumph and his loss,
  Like her, — because they love him.

By Francis Turner Palgrave.

A STORY OF NAPLES.

ANCIEN RÉGIME.

AGAINST the long quays of Naples
    The long waves heave and sink,
And blaze in emerald showers,
    And melt in pearls on the brink.

But as towards Pausilippo
    By Margellina we go,
The crimson breath of the mountain
    Makes blood in the ripples below.

A stone lies there in the pavement.
    With a square cut into the stone ;
And our feet will carelessly cross it,
    Like a thousand more, and pass on.

But one clothed in widow's clothing
    Like a veiled Vestal stands,
And from that slab in the pavement
    Warns with imperious hands.

Smiling the sentinels watch us ;
    A smile and a sneer in one ;
And that lordly woman bends her,
    And wipes the dust from the stone.

'What secret is in that service
  Which she does like a thing divine?
Why guards she the stone from footsteps,
  Like a priestess guarding a shrine?'

As a wild thing stabbed by the hunters
  She turned on us quickly and rose:
'Oh, ye who pass and behold me,
  Why ask ye my grief of foes?

'It is enough to have borne them:
  It is enough to have lost:
My sons! My fair, fair children!
  Silence beseemeth most.

'Nor any woe like my woe
  Since the Just One was crucified,
And his Mother stood and beheld him,
  And could not die when he died.'

With that again she bowed her,
  And levelled her head with the stone;
And in the high noon silence
  We heard the mountain groan.

As whom a magic circle
  Traced round holds prisoner,
We stood and watched her kneeling,
  And could not speak or stir.

Then from her feet unbended
  She slowly rose to her height,
Through the worn robe appearing
  Like a queen in her own despite.

She knotted her hands behind her
  In a knot of bloodless gray,
As if so her lips unaided
  Alone her story should say.

Like the keen thrilling music
  Blown from a tongue of flame,
Through her lips that whispered story
  With a thin clear calmness came.

'In this square of dust-choked socket
  A beam was set last year;
And the scaffold shot forth above it
  The gliding axe to rear.

'With gaunt grim poles in order,
  As when men a palace build, —
'T is the house of King Death, this palace,
  With headsmen for courtiers filled!

'I come at daybreak often,
  And call it up in my brain:
I see the steel uplifted;
  I see it fall again.

'Sirs, 't was a morn like this morn,
  So white and lucid and still;
Only the scowl of thunder
  Sat on the face of the hill.

'The steel like the star of morning
  Hung silver-glittering on high:
It fell like the star of morning
  By God's hand struck from the sky.

' It rose with a gleam of crimson,
   And sank again as it rose:
And I stood here as one standing
   To watch the death of his foes.

' And your eyes may well look wonder
   That mine looked on that thing of hell!
And unasked ye know already
   Who died when lead-like it fell.

' Yes! they were fair as the morning,
   Those two young sons of my youth;
Stamped with the stamp of Nature, —
   From boyhood soldiers of truth.

' Soldiers of truth and of Italy;
   Her blood was quick in their veins,
As they writhed 'neath the lies that bound them,
   The canker-poisonous chains.

' The coarse-lipped Austrian tyrant,
   Our serf-kings holding in pay,
Keeps Italy weak and sundered,
   For the greater ease of his sway.

' In the farce they name our country
   A boot toward Africa thrust:
'T is a boot with an iron heel, then,
   To tread her own self in the dust.

' The priest-king haunts in the centre
   The eternal ruin of Rome;
The German tramples the Lombard;
   And here — is the Bourbon home.

'They saw these things, my fair ones!
    The beauty, the curse, and the woe:
The beauty that seems of heaven,
    The curse, pit-black from below.

'O Italy, mother of nations,
    Like her own fair sea-nymph's brood.
Who turn and rend their mother, —
    Children by name, not blood!

'A dubious intricate quarrel
    Broke from the court of the North;
And on some mission of order
    From Trent the columns pushed forth.

'They came down by Garigliano;
    At Teano their halt they called,
When the pomegranates were as carbuncles,
    And the stream-pools as emerald.

'A cry went up from our people,
    Volunteering by fifties to go;
And the king must come forth and lead them
    Against his ally the foe.

'E'en in the palace recesses
    The gold-lace conscience was stirred;
But the calmer confessor wisdom
    In season whispered a word.

'Sirs, from your land of freedom
    Ye cannot fathom our land!
They march out by Pausilippo,
    That flame-faced patriot band.

'The second son of a second
    Cousin of the blood at their head;
— Our gay volunteers to conquest,
    Oh, they were right royally led!

'But what, think you, was the conquest
    To which they were marched along,
And the deep rich oily *Te Deum*
    By the barytone cannon sung?

'— Where the road turns under Teano,
    Half behind the pomegranate close,
Red faced and stalwart-fashioned,
    Point-blank they came on their foes.

'Who should hold back the lions
    When the prey to their hands is given?
Each poised his musket and shouted
    As if at the sight of Heaven.

'And when that royal field-marshal
    With a *Halt!* fell back to the rear,
Who could rein in their onset,
    Or sever prudence from fear?

'Or care how the royal columns
    Ebbed slowly behind away,
While the best young blood of the city
    Unaided rushed to the fray?

'Ah! thrice blessed who fell forward
    Before the Tyrolean gun,
And gasped out their life in crimson,
    Beneath the crimson sun!

'Oh that I must live to say it,
  And live to say it in vain, —
My sons! my own two fair ones!
  Better had ye been slain.

'I saw them go forth at morning;
  I saw them not at night:
And yet they returned to the city
  As captives captured in fight.

'Sirs, the gold-laced thing in the palace,
  With a bestial instinct dim,
Knew that the soldiers of freedom
  Must be foes in heart to him.

'I said, the ways of the Bourbon
  Ye could not understand.
  They were carted hither as rebels
For a broken word of command.

'They had gone onward as lions
  When Royalty muttered *Withdraw!*
And their lives at once lay forfeit
  At the lawless feet of the law.

'In the black Castel del Movo
  They lodged them side by side;
And between them, — a Tyrolese soldier
  For order and peace to provide.

'That square above is the window,
  Notched on the white wall stone;'
We looked: and again in the silence
  We heard the mountain groan.

' Sirs, for this king my husband
   In youth laid his own life down !
And I prayed their lives might be spared me,
   Their palace pass to the crown.

' How should I do but ask it ?
   — Yet better not to have asked,
Had I seen 'neath a face of mercy
   Hell's particular malice masked.

' Ye have heard how between two mothers
   King Solomon judged of old :
But how between her two children
   Could a mother such judgment hold ?

' One life, they said, was given me ;
   And I was to choose the one :
— The message came at even,
   And I sat till the night was done :

' And I know not how they went by me,
   The long, long day and the night ;
Only within my forehead
   Was a burning spot of light :

' And a cry, *My brother ! my brother !*
   Why art thou taken from me ?
O choice unjust and cruel !
   Would that I had died for thee !

' I could not answer the message ;
   I could not think or pray :
Only I saw within me
   That burning spot alway.

' Poison and glare together,
  Like the wormwood star of Saint John,
It sat within my temples,
  Throbbing and smouldering on.

' Then once with odor and freshness,
  As of field in summer rain,
The vision of their sweet childhood
  Was borne on my aching brain.

' Bent over one book together
  I saw the fair heads of the twain ;
As they read how in Roman battle
  Brother by brother was slain.

' And their heads are closer together,
  Their hands clasp o'er and o'er,
As they swear that death the divider
  Shall only unite them more.

' — Toll ! toll ! and again !
  A bell broke forth in the air :
And I looked out on the morning;
  And the morning was still and fair.

' A black flag hung from the castle,
  Where the thin bare flagstaff stands.
And I thought to go up to the castle
  With that bitter choice in my hands.

' A timid crowd was pressing,
  And bore me along the street,
And I saw the tall scaffold standing
  Upon these flags at our feet.

' I saw the steel descending
  As a star runs down from the sky :
— Why should I tell the story ?
  Ye know it as well as I !

'   The axe took both as I wavered
  Upon that choice accursed !
Now am I wholly childless —
  I know not which is worst.

' My sons ! My fair, fair children !
  I know not where they lie :
Only I know that together
  They died, — and I could not die.'

— A fork of flame from Vesuvius
  Through his black cone went on high ;
And a cloud branched out like a pine-tree
  With thunders throned in the sky.

The crimson breath of the mountain
  Made blood in the ripples below :
But she stood gray as marble,
  In Niobean woe.

And like a Roman matron
  O'er her face she folded the veil,
With a more fixed composure
  Than we who heard her tale.

By Francis Bret Harte.

DICKENS IN CAMP.

ABOVE the pines the moon was slowly drifting,
　　The river sang below ;
The dim Sierras, far beyond, uplifting
　　Their minarets of snow.

The roaring camp-fire, with rude humor, painted
　　The ruddy tints of health
On haggard face and form that drooped and fainted
　　In the fierce race for wealth ;

Till one arose, and from his pack's scant treasure
　　A hoarded volume drew,
And cards were dropped from hands of listless leisure
　　To hear the tale anew ;

And then, while round them shadows gathered faster,
　　And as the twilight fell,
He read aloud the book wherein the Master
　　Had writ of ' Little Nell.'

Perhaps 't was boyish fancy, — for the reader
　　Was youngest of them all, —
But, as he read, from clustering pine and cedar
　　A silence seemed to fall ;

The fir-trees, gathering closer in the shadows,
  Listened in every spray,
While the whole camp, with ' Nell ' on English meadows,
  Wandered and lost their way.

And so in mountain solitudes — o'ertaken
  As by some spell divine — -
Their cares dropped from them like the needles shaken
  From out the gusty pine.

Lost is that camp, and wasted all its fire :
  And he who wrought that spell? - -
Ah, towering pine and stately Kentish spire,
  Ye have one tale to tell !

Lost is that camp ! but let its fragrant story
  Blend with the breath that thrills
With hop-vines' incense all the pensive glory
  That fills the Kentish hills.

And on that grave where English oak and holly
  And laurel wreaths entwine,
Deem it not all a too presumptuous folly, —
  This spray of Western pine !

By George Walter Thornbury.

THE DEATH OF TH' OWD SQUIRE.

'T was a wild, mad kind of night, as black as the bottom-
    less pit,
The wind was howling away, like a Bedlamite in a fit,
Tearing the ash-boughs off, and mowing the poplars down,
In the meadows beyond the old flour-mill, where you turn
    off to the town.

And the rain (well, it *did* rain) dashing the window-glass,
And deluging on the roof, as the devil were come to pass ;
The gutters were running in floods outside the stable door,
And the spouts splashed from the tiles, as if they would
    never give o'er.

Lor' ! how the winders rattled ! You 'd almost ha' thought
    that thieves
Were wrenching at the shutters, while a ceaseless pelt of
    leaves
Flew at the door in gusts ; and I could hear the beck
Calling so loud, I knew at once it was up to a tall man's
    neck.

We was huddling in the harness-room, by a little scrap of
    fire,
And Tom, the coachman, he was there, a-practising for the
    choir ;

But it sounded desmal, anthem did, for Squire was dying
    fast,
And the doctor 'd said, do what he would, 'Squire's break-
    ing up at last.'

The death-watch, sure enough, ticked loud just over th'
    owd man's head,
Though he had never once been heard up there since mas-
    ter's boy lay dead;
And the only sound, beside Tom's toon, was the stirring
    in the stalls,
And the gnawing and the scratching of the rats in the owd
    walls.

We could n't hear Death's foot pass by, but we knew that
    he was near;
And the chill rain, and the wind and cold, made us all
    shake with fear;
We listened to the clock upstairs, — 't was breathing soft
    and low,
For the nurse said at the turn of night the old Squire's
    soul must go.

Master had been a wildish man and led a roughish life;
Did n't he shoot the Bowton Squire, who dared write to
    his wife?
He beat the Rads at Hindon town, I heard, in Twenty-nine,
When every pail in market-place was brimmed with red
    port wine.

And as for hunting, bless your soul! why, for forty year
    or more
He 'd kept the Marley hounds, man, as his fayther did afore;

6

And now to die, and in his bed — the season just begun —
It made him fret, the doctors said, as 't might do any one.

And when the young sharp lawer came to see him sign his
     will,
Squire made me blow my horn outside as we was going to
     kill;
And we turned the hounds out in the court, – that seemed
     to do him good;
For he swore, and sent us off to seek a fox in Thornhill
     Wood.

But then the fever it rose high, and he would go see the
     room
Where Missus died ten years ago when Lammastide shall
     come :
I mind the year, because our mare at Salisbury broke
     down;
Moreover the town hall was burnt at Steeple Deiston
     town.

It might be two, or half-past two, the wind seemed quite
     asleep;
Tom, he was off, but I awake sat, watch and ward to keep;
The moon was up, quite glorious like, the rain no longer
     fell,
When all at once out clashed and clanged the rusty turret
     bell,

That had n't been heard for twenty year, not since the
     Luddite days;
Tom he leapt up, and I leapt up, for all the house ablaze

Had sure not scared us half as much; and out we ran like
    mad, —
I, Tom, and Joe, the whipper-in, an t' little stable lad.

'He's killed hisself,' that's the idea that came into my
    head;
I felt as sure as though I saw Squire Barrowby was dead;
When all at once a door flew back, and he met us face to
    face;
His scarlet coat was on his back, and he looked like the
    old race.

The nurse was clinging to his knees, and crying like a
    child;
The maids were sobbing on the stairs, for he looked fierce
    and wild:
'Saddle me Lightning Bess, my man,' that's what he said
    to me;
'The moon is up, we're sure to find at Stop or Etterby.

'Get out the hounds; I'm well to-night, and young again
    and sound;
I'll have a run once more before they put me under-
    ground:
They brought my father home feet first, and it never shall
    be said
That his son Joe, who rode so straight, died quietly in his
    bed.

'Brandy!' he cried; 'a tumbler-full, you women howling
    there!'
Then clapped the old black velvet cap upon his long gray
    hair,

Thrust on his boots, snatched down his whip; though he
    was old and weak,
There was a devil in his eye that would not let me speak.

We loosed the hounds to humor him, and sounded on the
    horn:
The moon was up above the woods, just east of Haggard
    Bourne;
I buckled Lightning's throat-lash fast; the Squire was
    watching me;
He let the stirrups down himself, so quick, yet carefully.

Then up he got and spurred the mare, and ere I well could
    mount,
He drove the yard gate open, man, and called to old Dick
    Blount,
Our huntsman, dead five years ago — for the fever rose
    again,
And was spreading, like a flood of flame, fast up into his
    brain.

Then off he flew before the hounds, yelling to call us on,
While we stood there, all pale and dumb, scarce knowing
    he was gone;
We mounted, and below the hill we saw the fox break out,
And down the covert ride we heard the old Squire's part-
    ing shout.

And in the moonlit meadow mist we saw him fly the rail
Beyond the hurdles by the beck, just half-way down the
    vale;

I saw him breast fence after fence — nothing could turn
    him back ;
And in the moonlight after him streamed out the brave old
    pack.

'T was like a dream, Tom cried to me, as we rode free and
    fast ;
Hoping to turn him at the brook, that could not well be
    past,
For it was swollen with the rain ; but Lord ! 't was not
    to be ;
Nothing could stop old Lightning Bess but the broad
    breast of the sea.

The hounds swept on, and well in front the mare had got
    her stride ;
She broke across the fallow land that runs by the down
    side ;
We pulled up on Chalk Linton Hill, and as we stood us
    there,
Two fields beyond we saw the Squire fall stone dead from
    the mare.

Then she swept on, and, in full cry, the hounds went out
    of sight ;
A cloud came over the broad moon, and something dimmed
    our sight,
As Tom and I bore master home, both speaking under
    breath,
And that 's the way I saw th' owd Squire ride boldly to his
    death.

By Henry Austin Dobson.

BEFORE SEDAN.

'The dead hand clasped a letter.'

Special Correspondence.

HERE, in this leafy place,
  Quiet he lies,
Cold, with his sightless face
  Turned to the skies;
'T is but another dead:
All you can say is said.

Carry his body hence, —
  Kings must have slaves;
Kings climb to eminence
  Over men's graves:
So this man's eye is dim, —
Throw the earth over him.

What was the white you touched,
  There, at his side?
Paper his hand had clutched
  Tight ere he died, —
Message or wish, may be;
Smooth the folds out and see.

Hardly the worst of us
   Here could have smiled!
Only the tremulous
   Words of a child, —
Prattle, that has for stops
Just a few ruddy drops.

Look. 'She is sad to miss,
   Morning and night,
His — her dead father's — kiss ;
   Tries to be bright,
Good to mamma and sweet :'
That is all. 'Marguerite.'

Ah, if beside the dead
   Slumbered the pain!
Ah, if the hearts that bled
   Slept with the slain!
If the grief died, — but no, —
Death will not have it so.

By Robert Buchanan.

THE BALLAD OF JUDAS ISCARIOT.

'T WAS the body of Judas Iscariot
   Lay in the Field of Blood ;
'T was the soul of Judas Iscariot
   Beside the body stood.

Black was the earth by night,
   And black was the sky ;
Black, black were the broken clouds,
   Though the red moon went by.

'T was the body of Judas Iscariot
   Strangled and dead lay there ;
'T was the soul of Judas Iscariot
   Looked on it in despair.

The breath of the World came and went
   Like a sick man's in rest ;
Drop by drop on the World's eyes
   The dews fell cool and blest.

Then the soul of Judas Iscariot
   Did make a gentle moan, —
' I will bury underneath the ground
   My flesh and blood and bone.

' I will bury deep beneath the soil,
   Lest mortals look thereon,
And when the wolf and raven come
   The body will be gone !

' The stones of the field are sharp as steel,
   And hard and cold, God wot ;
And I must bear my body hence
   Until I find a spot ! '

'T was the soul of Judas Iscariot,
   So grim and gaunt and gray,
Raised the body of Judas Iscariot,
   And carried it away.

And as he bare it from the field
   Its touch was cold as ice,
And the ivory teeth within the jaw
   Rattled aloud, like dice.

As the soul of Judas Iscariot
   Carried its load with pain,
The Eye of Heaven, like a lanthorn's eye,
   Opened and shut again.

Half he walked, and half he seemed
   Lifted on the cold wind ;
He did not turn, for chilly hands
   Were pushing from behind.

The first place that he came unto
   It was the open wold,
And underneath were prickly whins,
   And a wind that blew so cold.

The next place that he came unto
  It was a stagnant pool,
And when he threw the body in
  It floated light as wool.

He drew the body on his back,
  And it was dripping chill,
And the next place he came unto
  Was a Cross upon a hill :

A Cross upon the windy hill,
  And a Cross on either side,
Three skeletons that swing thereon,
  Who had been crucified.

And on the middle cross-bar sat
  A white dove slumbering ;
Dim it sat in the dim light,
  With its head beneath its wing.

And underneath the middle Cross
  A grave yawned wide and vast,
But the soul of Judas Iscariot
  Shivered, and glided past.

The fourth place that he came unto
  It was the Brig of Dread,
And the great torrents rushing down
  Were deep and swift and red.

He dared not fling the body in
  For fear of faces dim,
And arms were waved in the wild water
  To thrust it back to him.

'T was the soul of Judas Iscariot
  Turned from the Brig of Dread,
And the dreadful foam of the wild water
  Had splashed the body red.

For days and nights he wandered on
  Upon an open plain,
And the days went by like blinding mist,
  And the nights like rushing rain.

For days and nights he wandered on,
  All through the Wood of Woe;
And the nights went by like moaning wind,
  And the days like drifting snow.

'T was the soul of Judas Iscariot
  Came with a weary face, —
Alone, alone, and all alone,
  Alone in a lonely place.

He wandered east, he wandered west,
  And heard no human sound;
For months and years, in grief and tears,
  He wandered round and round.

For months and years, in grief and tears,
  He walked the silent night;
Then the soul of Judas Iscariot
  Perceived a far-off light, —

A far-off light across the waste,
  As dim as dim might be,
That came and went, like the lighthouse gleam
  On a black night at sea.

'T was the soul of Judas Iscariot
　　Crawled to the distant gleam;
And the rain came down, and the rain was blown
　　Against him with a scream.

For days and nights he wandered on,
　　Pushed on by hands behind;
And the days went by like black, black rain,
　　And the nights like rushing wind.

'T was the soul of Judas Iscariot,
　　Strange, and sad, and tall,
Stood all alone at dead of night
　　Before a lighted hall.

And the wold was white with snow,
　　And his foot-marks black and damp,
And the ghost of the silvern Moon arose,
　　Holding her yellow lamp.

And the icicles were on the eaves,
　　And the walls were deep with white,
And the shadows of the guests within
　　Passed on the window light.

The shadows of the wedding guests
　　Did strangely come and go,
And the body of Judas Iscariot
　　Lay stretched along the snow.

The body of Judas Iscariot
　　Lay stretched along the snow;
'T was the soul of Judas Iscariot
　　Ran swiftly to and fro.

To and fro and up and down,
  He ran so swiftly there,
As round and round the frozen Pole
  Glideth the lean white bear.

'T was the Bridegroom sat at the table-head,
  And the lights burnt bright and clear.
' Oh, who is that,' the Bridegroom said,
  ' Whose weary feet I hear ? '

'T was one looked from the lighted hall,
  And answered soft and slow :
' It is a wolf runs up and down
  With a black track in the snow.'

The Bridegroom in his robe of white
  Sat at the table-head.
' Oh, who is that who moans without ? '
  The blessèd Bridegroom said.

'T was one looked from the lighted hall,
  And answered fierce and low,
' 'T is the soul of Judas Iscariot
  Gliding to and fro.'

'T was the soul of Judas Iscariot
  Did hush itself and stand,
And saw the Bridegroom at the door
  With a light in his hand.

The Bridegroom stood in the open door,
  And he was clad in white,
And far within the Lord's Supper
  Was spread so broad and bright.

The Bridegroom shaded his eyes and looked,
And his face was bright to see.
' What dost thou here at the Lord's Supper
With thy body's sins ? ' said he.

'T was the soul of Judas Iscariot
Stood black and sad and bare :
' I have wandered many nights and days ;
There is no light elsewhere.'

'T was the wedding guests cried out within,
And their eyes were fierce and bright :
' Scourge the soul of Judas Iscariot
Away into the night ! '

The Bridegroom stood in the open door,
And he waved hands still and slow,
And the third time that he waved his hands
The air was thick with snow.

And of every flake of falling snow,
Before it touched the ground,
There came a dove, and a thousand doves
Made sweet sound.

'T was the body of Judas Iscariot
Floated away full fleet,
And the wings of the doves that bare it off
Were like its winding-sheet.

'T was the Bridegroom stood at the open door
And beckoned, smiling sweet ;
'T was the soul of Judas Iscariot
Stole in, and fell at his feet.

' The Holy Supper is spread within,
 And the many candles shine,
And I have waited long for thee
 Before I poured the wine ! '

The supper wine is poured at last,
 The lights burn bright and fair ;
Iscariot washes the Bridegroom's feet,
 And dries them with his hair.

By William Bell Scott.

WOODSTOCK MAZE.

'Oh, never shall any one find you then!'
    Said he, merrily pinching her cheek;
'But why?' she asked, — he only laughed, —
    'Why shall it be thus, now speak!'
'Because so like a bird art thou,
    Thou must live within green trees,
With nightingales and thrushes and wrens,
    And the humming of wild bees.'
        Oh, the shower and the sunshine every day
        Pass and pass, be ye sad, be ye gay.

'Nay, nay, you jest; no wren am I,
    Nor thrush nor nightingale,
And rather would keep this arras and wall
    'Tween me and the wind's assail.
I like to hear little Minnie's gay laugh,
    And the whistle of Japes the page,
Or to watch old Madge when her spindle twirls,
    And she tends it like a sage.'
        Oh, the leaves, brown, yellow, and red, still fall,
        Fall and fall over churchyard or hall.

'Yea, yea, but thou art the world's best Rose,
    And about thee flowers I'll twine,
And wall thee round with holly and beech,
    Sweet-briar and jessamine.'

' Nay, nay, sweet master, I 'm no Rose,
  But a woman indeed, indeed,
And love many things both great and small,
  And of many things more take heed.'
    Oh, the shower and the sunshine every day
    Pass and pass, be ye sad, be ye gay.

' Aye, sweetheart, sure thou sayest sooth,
  I think thou art even so!
But yet needs must I dibble the hedge,
  Close serried as hedge can grow.
Then Minnie and Japes and Madge shall be
  Thy merry-mates all day long,
And thou shalt hear my bugle-call
  For matin or even-song.'
    Oh, the leaves, brown, yellow, and red, still fall,
    Fall and fall over churchyard or hall.

' Look yonder now, my blue-eyed bird,
  Seest thou aught by yon far stream?
There shalt thou find a more curious nest
  Than ever thou sawest in dream.'
She followed his finger, she looked in vain,
  She saw neither cottage nor hall,
But at his beck came a litter on wheels,
  Screened by a red silk caul ;
He lifted her in by her lily-white hand,
  So left they the blithe sunny wall.
    Oh, the shower and the sunshine every day
    Pass and pass, be ye sad, be ye gay.

7

The gorse and ling are netted and strong,
  The conies leap everywhere,
The wild briar-roses by runnels grow thick;
  Seems never a pathway there.
Then come the dwarf oaks knotted and wrung,
  Breeding apples and mistletoe,
And now tall elms from the wet mossed ground
  Straight up to the white clouds go.
    Oh, the leaves, brown, yellow, and red, still fall,
    Fall and fall over churchyard or hall.

' O weary hedge, O thorny hedge ! '
  Quoth she in her lonesome bower,
' Round and round it is all the same ;
  Days, weeks, have all one hour ;
I hear the cushat far overhead,
  From the dark heart of that plane ;
Sudden rushes of wings I hear,
  And silence as sudden again.
    Oh, the shower and the sunshine every day
    Pass and pass, be ye sad, be ye gay.

' Maiden Minnie she mopes by the fire,
  Even now in the warmth of June ;
I like not Madge to look in my face,
  Japes now hath never a tune.
But oh, he is so kingly strong,
  And oh, he is kind and true ;
Shall not my babe, if God cares for me,
  Be his pride and his joy too ?
    Oh, the leaves, brown, yellow, and red, still fall,
    Fall and fall over churchyard or hall.

' I lean my faint heart against this tree
  Whereon he hath carved my name,
I hold me up by this fair bent bough,
  For he held once by the same ;
But everything here is dank and cold,
  The daisies have sickly eyes,
The clouds like ghosts down into my prison
  Look from the barred-out skies.
    Oh, the shower and the sunshine every day
    Pass and pass, be ye sad, be ye gay.

' I tune my lute and I straight forget
  What I minded to play, woe 's me !
Till it feebly moans to the sharp short gusts
  Aye rushing from tree to tree.
Often that single redbreast comes
  To the sill where my Jesu stands ;
I speak to him as to a child; he flies,
  Afraid of these poor thin hands !
    Oh, the leaves, brown, yellow, and red, still fall,
    Fall and fall over churchyard or hall.

' The golden evening burns right through
  My dark chamber windows twain :
I listen, all round me is only a grave,
  Yet listen I ever again.
Will he come ? I pluck the flower-leaves off,
  And at each, cry, yes, no, yes !·
I blow the down from the dry hawkweed,
  Once, twice, ah ! it flyeth amiss !
    Oh, the shower and the sunshine every day
    Pass and pass, be ye sad, be ye gay.

' Hark ! he comes ! yet his footstep sounds
   As it sounded never before !
Perhaps he thinks to steal on me,
   But I 'll hide behind the door.'
She ran, she stopped, stood still as stone —
   It was Queen Eleänore ;
And at once she felt that it was death
   The hungering she-wolf bore !
     Oh, the leaves, brown, yellow, and red, still fall,
     Fall and fall over churchyard or hall.

By Richard Hengist Horne.

HAJARLIS.

A TRAGIC BALLAD, SET TO AN OLD ARABIAN AIR.

I LOVED Hajarlis, and was loved,
  Both children of the Desert, we;
And deep as were her lustrous eyes,
  My image ever could I see.

And in my heart she also shone,
  As doth a star above a well;
And we each other's thoughts enjoyed,
  As camels listen to a bell.

A Sheik unto Hajarlis came,
  And said, 'Thy beauty fires my dreams!
Young Ornab spurn, fly to my tent;
  So shalt thou walk in golden beams.'

But from the Sheik my maiden turned,
  And he was wroth with her and me:
Hajarlis down a pit was lowered,
  And I was fastened to a tree.

Nor bread, nor water, had she there;
  But oft a slave would come and go;
O'er the pit bent he, muttering words,
  And aye took back the unvarying 'No!'

The simoom came with sullen glare ; —
  Breathed desert mysteries through my tree !
I only heard the starving sighs
  From that pit's mouth unceasingly.

Day after day, night after night,
  Hajarlis' famished moans I hear !
And then I prayed her to consent,
  For *my* sake, in my wild despair.

Calm strode the Sheik, looked down the pit,
  And said, ' Thy beauty now is gone ;
Thy last moans will thy lover hear,
  While thy slow torments feed my scorn.'

They spared me that I still might know
  Her thirst and frenzy, till at last
The pit was silent; and I felt
  Her life, and mine, were with the past !

A friend that night cut through my bonds :
  The Sheik amidst his camels slept;
We fired his tent, and drove them in,
  And then with joy I screamed and wept;

And cried, ' A spirit comes arrayed,
  From that dark pit, in golden beams !
Thy slaves are fled, thy camels mad;
  Hajarlis once more fires thy dreams ! '

The camels blindly trod him down,
  While still we drove them o'er his bed;
Then with a stone I beat his breast,
  As I would smite him ten times dead !

I dragged him far out on the sands :
  And vultures came, a screaming shoal!
And while they fanged and flapped, I prayed
  Great Allah to destroy his soul !

And day and night again I sat
  Above that pit, and thought I heard
Hajarlis' moans ; and cried, ' My *love !* '
  With heart still breaking at each word.

Is it the night-breeze in my ear
  That wooes me like a fanning dove ?
Is it herself ? — O desert-sands,
  Enshroud me ever with thy love !

By Robert Browning.

HERVE RIEL.

On the sea and at the Hogue, sixteen hundred ninety-two,
  Did the English fight the French, — woe to France!
And, the thirty-first of May, helter-skelter through the blue,
Like a crowd of frightened porpoises a shoal of sharks
      pursue,
  Came crowding ship on ship to St. Malo on the Rance,
With the English fleet in view.
'T was the squadron that escaped, with the victor in full
      chase,
    First and foremost of the drove, in his great ship,
      Damfreville;
      Close on him fled, great and small,
      Twenty-two good ships in all;
And they signalled to the place,
'Help the winners of a race!
    Get us guidance, give us harbor, take us quick, — or,
      quicker still,
    Here's the English can and will!'

Then the pilots of the place put out brisk and leaped on
      board.
    'Why, what hope or chance have ships like these to
      pass?' laughed they;

' Rocks to starboard, rocks to port, all the passage scarred
    and scored,
Shall the " Formidable " here with her twelve and eighty
    guns,
  Think to make the river-mouth by the single narrow
    way,
Trust to enter where 't is ticklish for a craft of twenty tons,
    And with flow at full beside ?
    Now 't is slackest ebb of tide.
  Reach the mooring ?   Rather say,
While rock stands or water runs,
  Not a ship will leave the bay ! '

Then was called a council straight ;
Brief and bitter the debate :
' Here 's the English at our heels ; would you have them
    take in tow
All that 's left us of the fleet, linked together stern and
    bow,
  For a prize to Plymouth Sound ?
  Better run the ships aground ! '
  (Ended Damfreville his speech,)
  ' Not a minute more to wait !
  Let the captains all and each
  Shove ashore, then blow up, burn the vessels on the
    beach !
France must undergo her fate.'

' Give the word ! '   But no such word
Was ever spoke or heard ;
  For up stood, for out stepped, for in struck amid all
    these,

A captain ? A lieutenant? A mate, — first, second, third ?
   No such man of mark, and meet
   With his betters to compete !
  But a simple Breton sailor pressed by Tourville for
    the fleet, —
A poor coasting-pilot he, Hervé Riel the Croisickese.

And, ' What mockery or malice have we here ? ' cries
   Hervé Riel :
' Are you mad, you Malouins ? Are you cowards, fools, or
   rogues ?
Talk to me of rocks and shoals, me who took the soundings,
   tell
On my fingers every bank, every shallow, every swell
  'Twixt the offing here and Grève, where the river dis-
   embogues?
Are you bought by English gold? Is it love the lying 's
   for ?
   Morn and eve, night and day,
   Have I piloted your bay,
Entered free and anchored fast at the fort of Solidor.
   Burn the fleet and ruin France? That were worse than
    fifty Hogues !
    Sirs, they know I speak the truth ! Sirs, believe me,
    there 's a way !
Only let me lead the line,
   Have the biggest ship to steer,
   Get this " Formidable " clear,
Make the others follow mine,
And I lead them most and least by a passage I know
   well,

Right to Solidor, past Grève,
  And there lay them safe and sound;
And if one ship misbehave, —
  Keel so much as grate the ground, —
Why, I 've nothing but my life; here 's my head!' cries
  Hervé Riel.

Not a minute more to wait.
' Steer us in, then, small and great !
  Take the helm, lead the line, save the squadron !' cried
    its chief.
Captains, give the sailor place !
  He is Admiral, in brief.
Still the north-wind, by God's grace !
See the noble fellow's face
As the big ship, with a bound,
Clears the entry like a hound,
Keeps the passage as its inch of way were the wide sea's
    profound !
  See. safe through shoal and rock,
  How they follow in a flock,
Not a ship that misbehaves, not a keel that grates the
    ground,
  Not a spar that comes to grief !
The peril, see, is past,
All are harbored to the last ;
And just as Hervé Riel halloos ' Anchor !' — sure as fate,
Up the English come, too late.

So the storm subsides to calm ;
  They see the green trees wave
  On the heights o'erlooking Grève :

Hearts that bled are stanched with balm.
' Just our rapture to enhance,
    Let the English rake the bay,
Gnash their teeth and glare askance
    As they cannonade away !
'Neath rampired Solidor pleasant riding on the Rance !'
How hope succeeds despair on each captain's countenance !
Outburst all with one accord,
    ' This is Paradise for Hell !
    Let France, let France's King
    Thank the man that did the thing !'
What a shout, and all one word,
    ' Hervé Riel !'
As he stepped in front once more,
    Not a symptom of surprise
    In the frank blue Breton eyes,
Just the same man as before.

Then said Damfreville, ' My friend,
I must speak out at the end,
    Though I find the speaking hard.
Praise is deeper than the lips ;
You have saved the King his ships,
    You must name your own reward.
'Faith, our sun was near eclipse !
Demand whate'er you will,
France remains your debtor still.
Ask to heart's content, and have ! or my name 's not
        Damfreville.'

Then a beam of fun outbroke
On the bearded mouth that spoke,

As the honest heart laughed through
Those frank eyes of Breton blue :
'Since I needs must say my say,
Since on board the duty 's done,
    And from Malo Roads to Croisic Point, what is it but a
        run ?
Since 't is ask and have I may, —
    Since the others go ashore, —
Come ! a good whole holiday !
    Leave to go and see my wife, whom I call the Belle
        Aurore !'
    That he asked and that he got, — nothing more.

Name and deed alike are lost ;
Not a pillar nor a post
    In his Croisic keeps alive the feat as it befell ;
Not a head in white and black
On a single fishing-smack   •
In memory of the man but for whom had gone to wrack
    All that France saved from the fight whence England
        bore the bell.
Go to Paris : rank on rank
    Search the heroes flung pell-mell
On the Louvre, face and flank ;
    You shall look long enough ere you come to Hervé
        Riel.
So, for better and for worse,
Hervé Riel, accept my verse !
In my verse, Hervé Riel, do thou once more
Save the squadron, honor France, love thy wife, the Belle
    Aurore.

By Emily Pfeiffer.

THE GULF.

THE only son of the Count Lasserre
  Loved a maiden of low degree;
Her feet on the mountain wandered bare,
  A wing-clipt eagle was he.

He fed him full upon dead men's minds,
  Drained learning to the lees:
She knew the voices of the winds,
  The secret of the bees.

One day, as halting on the hill,
  His hard-drawn breath he took,
She met him with a wild-bird trill,
  Down leaping with the brook.

The brook came singing from its source,
  The maiden stopped half-way;
The brook went laughing on its course;
  It won the race that day!

The brook went singing to the vale,
  The maiden lingered there,
And listened to a wondrous tale, —
  The love of Raoul Lasserre.

A castle set on a rocky ridge
  Bore the arms of the Counts Lasserre;
A hut on a rifted mountain ledge
  Was the home of Frieda the fair.

The valley that yawned between the two
  In the morning mist showed white;
At noon the valley was heavenly blue,
  But was black as doom at night.

And the river that rolled in its stormy bed
  Murmured so far below,
You never could tell what the river said,
  If it sung of weal or of woe:

Though when glacier drifts had swelled its flood
  It rose as if in warning;
Still a rede will serve, as fits the mood,
  For counsel or for scorning.

So at morn, at noon, and eventide,
  In sunshine or in mist,
The twain that chasm did divide
  Still kept their faithful tryst:

He on the rock with castled crown,
  High over the world uplift;
She on the mound which seemed to frown
  Dark on the deadly rift.

There, face to face, when the day was clear,
  They stood and spake no word;
But through mist or murk each lover would hear,
  As the note of a wild wood bird.

There sometimes standing face to face,
 Their souls met on the wing:
Oh, then the valley, all choked with haze,
 Would seem but a lying thing!

And Raoul Lasserre would have followed his soul,
 And followed to body's death,
If the far-off river had ceased to roll
 Its warning from beneath.

Yet again when the fir-tops pierced the blue
 At noon on the mountain's side,
By the sinking of his heart he knew
 That the gulf was deep and wide;

And oft as he heard the wild bird's trill
 Across the cleft at night,
He curst the chasm that balked the will
 Of a man in love's despite.

To come of a race so proud, and eke
 Unbroken to suffer wrong,
Yet be forced to bow, in a body weak,
 To the mandate of the strong;

To be born and reared in an eagle's nest,
 Without an eagle's wing
To bear you aloft on an eagle's quest,
 Is a weary and doleful thing.

So faint and fainter grew Raoul Lasserre,
 And his eye took an angrier light
As he wound his way down his turret-stair
 At morn and noon and night.

Foul shame when a bodice that closely prest
  As the bark of the sapling beech,
Lies withering over a faithful breast,
  Like the coat of a blighted peach!

Oh, Frieda, maiden brave and pure,
  Take heed to where you go!
Your foot on the mountain slope is sure;
  It soils not the virgin snow;

Be it yours the golden dawn to greet
  With a step as free as air;
But you never may sit in my lady's seat,
  Or climb up the castle stair!

Young Raoul Lasserre was as good as dead,
  So sick and sore was he,
And for summer-long days had tost on a bed,
  As a bark on the raging sea.

But he rose when the breath of the glacier came
  And quickened him, spirit and flesh:
The glacier he called by the maiden's name,
  Whose soul was as pure and fresh.

The grapes were clustering on the wall,
  The apples burning red;
The sunflower looked above them all,
  The sun was overhead,

And Raoul crept to the trysting-place, —
  That autumn day was clear!
He could see the heart's blood flush the face
  That seemed, O God, how near!

He saw, and his heart went forth to her, —
    His heart that was bold and true.
Though the river thundered its hoarse demur,
    It leapt the chasm so blue.

And she, — she opened the strong white arms
    That had locked him safe in bliss,
And met him, she and her peasant charms, —
    They were good enough for this !

She opened her loving arms to save
    Her lover on the edge ;
He rose to her from the sobbing wave,
    As she sprung from her mountain ledge.

Now together, borne on the rushing tide,
    Their bodies to the sea
Drift on and on ; for the sea is wide,
    And recks not of degree.

By William Allingham.

LADY ALICE.

I.

Now what doth Lady Alice so late on the turret stair,
Without a lamp to light her, but the diamond in her hair;
When every arching passage overflows with shallow gloom,
And dreams float through the castle into every silent room?

She trembles at her footsteps, although they fall so light;
Through the turret loopholes she sees the wild midnight;
Broken vapors streaming across the stormy sky;
Down the empty corridors the blast doth moan and cry.

She steals along a gallery; she pauses by a door;
And fast her tears are dropping down upon the oaken
    floor;
And thrice she seems returning, but thrice she turns
    again, —
How heavy lies the cloud of sleep on that old father's
    brain!

Oh, well it were that *never* shouldst thou waken from thy
    sleep!
For wherefore should they waken, who waken but to weep?
No more, no more beside thy bed doth Peace a vigil keep,
But Woe, — a lion that awaits thy rousing for its leap.

II.

An afternoon of April, no sun appears on high,
But a moist and yellow lustre fills the deepness of the sky:
And through the castle-gateway, left empty and forlorn,
Along the leafless avenue an honored bier is borne.

They stop. The long line closes up like some gigantic
      worm ;
A shape is standing in the path, a wan and ghost-like form,
Which gazes fixedly; nor moves, nor utters any sound;
Then, like a statue built of snow, sinks down upon the
      ground.

And though her clothes are ragged, and though her feet
      are bare,
And though all wild and tangled falls her heavy silk-brown
      hair ;
Though from her eyes the brightness, from her cheeks the
      bloom is fled,
They know their Lady Alice, the darling of the dead.

With silence, in her own old room the fainting form they
      lay,
Where all things stand unaltered since the night she fled
      away :
But who, but who shall bring to life her father from the
      clay ?
But who shall give her back again her heart of a former
      day ?

By Richard Henry Stoddard.

THE PEARL OF THE PHILIPPINES.[3]

'I HEAR, Relempago, that you
Were once a famous fisherman,
Who at Negros, or Palawan,
Or maybe it was at Zèbou,
Found something precious in the sand,
A nugget washed there by the rain,
That slipped from your too eager hand,
And soon as found was lost again.
If it had been a pearl instead
(Why does your good wife shake her head?)
I could the story understand;
For I have known so many lost,
And once too often to my cost.
I trade in pearls; I buy and sell.
They say I know their value well.

'I have seen some large ones in my day,
Have heard of larger, — who shall say
How large these unseen pearls have been?
I don't believe in things unseen.
I hear there 's one now at Zèbou
That dwarfs a bird's egg, and outshines

The full moon in its purity.
What say you? is the story true?
And what's the pearl called? Let me see!
The pearl of all the Philippines.'

'Twas at Manilla, and the three
Sat in a shaded gallery
That looked upon the river, where
All sorts of sailing boats all day
Went skimming round, like gulls at play,
And made a busy picture there.
The speaker was — what no man knew,
Except a merchant; Jew with Jew,
A Turk with Turks, Parsee, Hindoo,
But still to one religion true,
And that was Trade; a pleasant guest,
Who knowing many things knew best
What governs men, for he was one
Whom many trusted, trusting none.
His host, Relempago, who heard
His questions with an inward shock,
Looked up, but answered not a word.
He was a native Tagaloc,
A man that was not past his prime,
And yet was old before his time.
His face was sad, his hair was grey,
His eyes on something far away.
His wife was younger, and less sad;
A Spanish woman, she was clad
As are the Tagal women; fair,
With all her dark abundant hair,

That was a wonder to behold,
Drawn from her face with pins of gold.

'You have not seen it, I perceive,'
Said the pearl-merchant, --- 'nor have I.
I 'd have to see it to believe,
And then would rather have you by.
There 's no such pearl.' 'You spoke of me !'
After a pause his host began : ---

' Yes ! I was once a fisherman,
And loved, though now I hate, the sea.
'T was twenty, thirty years ago,
And this good lady by my side
Had not been many moons a bride
Of poor but proud Relempago.
That I was poor she did not care ;
She let me love her, loved again.
She comes of the best blood of Spain ;
There is no better anywhere.
You see what I am.   As I said,
I cast my bread upon the sea,
Or from the sea I drew my bread,
What matter, so it came to me ?
We loved, were young, our wants were few :
The happiest pair in all Zébou !
At last a child, and what before
Seemed happiness was more and more
The thing it seemed, the dream come true.
You smile : I see you never knew
A father's pleasure in a child.' ---
' Pardon, my friend ! I never smiled ;

I am a father.   I have three
Sweet troubles that are dear to me,' —
' But ours was not a trouble, — no !'
Said simple, good Kelempago.
' It was the sweetest, dearest child !
So beautiful, so gay, so wild,
And yet so sensitive and shy,
And given to sudden, strange alarms :
I 've seen it in its mother's arms,
Bubbling with laughter, stop and sigh.
It was like neither in the face,
For we are dark, and that was fair ;
An infant of another race,
That, born not in their dwelling-place,
Left some poor woman childless there !
A bird that to our nest had flown,
A pearl that in our shell had grown,
We cherished it with double care.
It came to us as, legend says
(I know not if the tale be true),
Another child in other days
Came hither to depart no more,
Found one bright morning on the shore,
The Infant Jesus of Zébou.' —
'So you too had,' the merchant said,
With just a touch of quiet scorn, —
' What shall I say ? — a Krishna born,
But with no halo round its head.
What did you name the boy ?' — ' A girl,
Not boy, and therefore dearer, sweeter :
We called the infant Margarita,

For was she not our precious Pearl?
You who have children, as you say,
Can guess how much we loved the child,
Watching her growth from day to day,
Grave if she wept, but if she smiled
Delighted with her.   We were told
That we grew young as she grew old.
I used to make long voyages,
Before she came, in distant seas ;
But now I never left Zèbou,
For there the great pearl oysters grew
(And still may grow, for aught I know —
I speak of thirty years ago).
Though waves were rough and winds were high,
And fathoms down the sea was dark,
And there was danger from the shark,
I shrank from nothing then, for I
Was young and bold and full of life,
And had at home a loving wife,
A darling child, who ran to me,
Stretching her arms out when I came,
And kissed my cheek, and lisped my name,
And sat for hours upon my knee.
What happier sight was there to see ?
What happier life was there to be ?
I lived, my little Pearl ! in thee.
Oh, mother ! why did I begin ?'
He stopped, and closed his eyes with pain,
Either to keep his tears therein,
Or bring that vision back again.
'You tell him !'

                    ' Sir!' the lady said,
' My husband bids me tell the tale.
One day the child began to ail;
Its little cheek was first too red,
And then it was too deathly pale.
It burned with fever; inward flame
Consumed it, which no wind could cool;
We bathed it in a mountain pool,
And it was burning all the same.
The next day it was cold, so cold
No fire could warm it.   So it lay,
Not crying much, too weak to play,
And looking all the while so old.
So fond too of its father, — he,
Good man, was more to it than I;
The moment his light step drew nigh,
It would no longer stay with me.
I said to him, "The child will die!"
But he declared it should not be.'
'"T is true!' Relempago replied :
' I felt, if Margarita died,
My heart was broken. And I said,
" She shall not die till I have tried
Once more to save her!"   What to do?
Then something put into my head
The Infant Jesus of Zèbou.
" I 'll go to him: the Child Divine
Will save this only child of mine.
I will present him with a pearl,
And he will spare my little girl, —
The largest pearl that I can find,

The one that shall delight his mind.
The purest, best, I give to you,
O Infant Jesus of Zèbou!"
"T was morning when I made the vow,
And well do I remember now
How light my heart was when I ran
Down to the sea, a happy man!
All that I passed along the way,
The woods around me, and above
The plaintive cooing of the dove,
The rustling of the hidden snake,
And wild ducks swimming in the lake,
The hideous lizards large as men, —
Nothing, I think, escaped me then,
And nothing will escape to-day.
I reached the shore, untied my boat,
Sprang in, and was again afloat
Upon the wild and angry sea,
That must give up its pearls to me,
Its pearl of pearls! But where to go?
West of the island of Bojo,
Some six miles off, there was a view
Of the cathedral of Zèbou,
Beneath whose dome the Child Divine
Was waiting for that pearl of mine.
Thither I went, and anchored; there
Dived fathoms down, found rocks and sands,
But no pearl-oysters anywhere,
And so came up with empty hands.
Twice, thrice, and — nothing! "Cruel sea!
Where hast thou hid thy pearls from me?

But I will have them, nor depart
Until I have them, for my heart
Would break, and my dear child would die.
She shall not die!   What was that cry?
Only the eagle's scream on high.
Fear not, Relempago!"   Once more
Down, down, along the rocks and sands
I groped in darkness, tore my hands,
And rose with nothing, as before.
" O Infant Jesus of Zèbou!
I promised a great pearl to you:
Help me to find it!"   Down again!
It seemed forever, whirled and whirled,
The deep foundations of the world
Engulfed me and my mortal pain ;
But not forever, for the sea
That swallowed would not harbor me.
I rose again, I saw the sun,
I felt my dreadful task was done.
My desperate hands had wrenched away
A great pearl-oyster from its bed
And brought it to the light of day ;
Its ragged shell was dripping red, —
They bled so then.   But all was well,
For in the hollow of that shell
The pearl, pear-shaped and perfect, lay.
My child was saved!   No need to tell
How I rejoiced, and how I flew
To the cathedral of Zèbou,
For there the Infant Jesus stands,
And holds my pearl upon his hands.'

He ended.   The pearl-merchant said, —
' You found your daughter better? ' — ' No ! '
The wife of poor Relempago
Replied.   ' He found his daughter dead.'   -
' 'T was fate ! ' he answered. — ' No ! ' said she,
' 'T was God !   He gave the child to me ;
He took the child : and He knew best.
He reached and took it from my breast ;
And in His hand to-day it shines,
The Pearl of all the Philippines.'

By John Payne.

THE BALLAD OF ISOBEL.

I.

THE day is dead, the night draws on,
　The shadows gather fast :
'T is many an hour yet to the dawn,
　Till Hallow-tide be past.

Till Hallow-tide be past and sped,
　The night is full of fear ;
For then they say the restless dead
　Unto the live draw near.

Between the Saints' day and the Souls'
　The dead wake in the mould ;
The poor dead, in their grassy knolls
　They lie and are a-cold.

They think upon the live that sit
　And drink the Hallow-ale,
Whilst they lie stark within the pit,
　Nailed down with many a nail.

And sore they wonder if the thought
　Live in them of the dead ;
And sore with wish they are distraught
　To feel the firelight red.

The Ballad of Isobel.

Betwixt the day and yet the day
   The Saints' and Souls' divide,
The dead folk rise out of the clay
   And wander far and wide.

They wander o'er the sheeted snow,
   Chill with the frore of death,
Until they see the windows glow
   With the fire's ruddy breath.

And if the cottage door be fast
   And but the light win out,
All night, until their hour is past,
   The dead walk thereabout.

And all night long the live folk hear
   Their windy song of sighs,
And waken all for very fear,
   Until the white day rise.

But if the folk be piteous,
   And pity the poor dead
That weary in the narrow house,
   Upon the cold earth's bed,

They pile the peats upon the fire
   And leave the door ajar,
That so the rosy flame aspire
   To where the grey ghosts are.

And syne they sweep the cottage floor
   And set the hearthside chair:
The sad dead watch beside the door
   Till midnight still the air.

And then towards the friendly glow
　Come trooping in the dead :
Until the cocks for morning crow,
　They sit by the fire red.

II.

'Oh, I have wearied long enough !
　I 'll weary me no more ;
But I will watch for my dead love
　Till Hallow-tide be o'er.'

He set the door across the sill ;
　The moonlight fluttered in :
The sad snow covered heath and hill,
　As far as eye could win.

The thin frost feathered in the air ;
　All dumb the white world lay ;
Night sat on it as cold and fair
　As death upon a may.

He turned him back into the room
　And sat him by the fire :
Night darkened round him in the gloom,
　The shadowtide rose higher.

He rose and looked out o'er the hill
　To where the grey kirk lay ;
The midnight quiet was so still,
　He heard the bell-chimes play.

Twelve times he heard the sweet bell chime ;
　No whit he stirred or spoke ;
But his eyes fixed, as if on Time
　The hour of judgment broke.

And as the last stroke fell and died,
  Over the kirkyard grey
Him seemed he saw a blue flame glide,
  Among the graves at play.

A flutter waved upon the breeze
  As of a spirit's wings:
A wind went by him through the trees,
  That spoke of heavenly things.

Him seemed he heard a sound of feet
  Upon the silver snow:
A rush of robes by him did fleet,
  A sighing soft and low.

He turned and sat him down again;
  The midnight filled the place:
The tears ran down like silent rain
  Upon his weary face.

'She will not come to me,' he said;
  'The death-swoon is too strong:
She hath forgot me with the dead, —
  Me that she loved so long.

'She will not come: she sleeps too sweet
  Within the quiet ground.
What worth is love, when life is fleet,
  And sleep in death so sound?

'She will not come!' — A soft cold air
  Upon his forehead fell:
He turned him to the empty chair;
  And there sat Isobel.

His dead love sat him side by side,
  His Minnie white and wan:
Within the tomb she could not bide,
  Whilst he sat weeping on.

Ah, wasted, wasted was her face,
  And sore her cheek was white :
But in her eyes the ancient grace
  Burnt with a feeble light.

Upon her breast the graveweed grey
  Fell to her little feet ;
But still the golden tresses lay
  About her bosom sweet.

'Ah, how is 't with ye, Isobel?
  How pale ye look and cold !
Ah, sore it is to think ye dwell
  Alone beneath the mould !

' Is 't weary for our love ye 've grown
  From dwelling with the dead,
Or shivering from the cold gravestone
  To find the firelight red?'

'Oh, 't is not that I 'm lorn of love,
  Or that a-cold I lie :
I trust in God that is above
  To bring you by and by.

' I feel your kisses on my face, --
  Your kisses sweet and warm :
Your love is in the burial-place ;
  I fear nor cold nor worm.

' I feel the love within your heart
  That beats for me alone :
I fear not change upon your part,
  Nor crave for the unknown.

· For to the dead no faint fears cling :
  All certainty have they :
They know (and smile at sorrowing)
  Love never dies away.

' No harm can reach me in Death's deep :
  It hath no fear for me :
God sweetens it to lie and sleep,
  Until His face I see.

' He makes it sweet to lie and wait
  Till we together meet,
And hand-in-hand athwart the gate
  Pass up the golden street.

' But where 's the babe that at my side
  Slept sweetly long ago?
So sore to me to-night it cried,
  I could not choose but go.

' I heard its voice so full of wail,
  It woke me in the grave :
Its sighs came to me on the gale,
  Across the wintry wave.

' For though death lap her wide and wild,
  A mother cannot rest
Except her little sucking child
  Be sleeping at her breast.'

' Ah, know'st thou not, my love ? ' he said,
  ' Methought the dead knew all,
When in that night of doom and dread
  The moving waters' wall

' Smote on our ship and drove it down
  Beneath the raging sea,
All of our company did drown,
  Alas ! save only me.

' And me the cruel billows cast
  Aswoon upon the strand ;
Thou dead within my arms held fast,
  Hand locked in other's hand.

' The ocean never to this day
  Gave up our baby dead :
Ah, woe is me that life should stay,
  When all its sweet is fled ! '

' Go down,' said she, ' to the seashore :
  God taketh ruth on thee :
Search well ; and I will come once more
  Ere yet the midnight be.'

She bent her sweet pale mouth to his :
  The snowdrift from the sky
Falls not so cold as did that kiss :
  He shook as he should die.

She looked on him with yearning eyes
  And vanished from his sight :
He heard the matin cock crow thrice ;
  The morning glimmered white.

III.

Then from his place he rose and sought
  The shore beside the sea :
And there all day he searched, but nought
  Until the eve found he.

At last a pale star glittered through
  The growing dusk of night,
And fell upon the waste of blue,
  A trembling wand of light.

And lo ! a wondrous thing befell :
  As though the small star's ray
Availed to break some year-old spell
  That on the water lay.

A white form rose out of the deep
  Where it so long had lain,
Cradled within the cold death-sleep :
  He knew his babe again.

It floated softly to his feet :
  White as a flower it lay :
God's love had kept its body sweet,
  Unravished of decay.

He thanked God weeping for His grace ;
  And many a tear he shed,
And many a kiss upon its face,
  That smiled as do the dead.

Then to the kirkyard where the maid
  Slept cold in clay he hied :
And with a loving hand he laid
  The baby by her side.

IV.

The dark fell down upon the earth ;
    Night held the quiet air :
He sat before the glowing hearth,
    Beside the empty chair.

Twelve times at last for middle night
    Rang out the kirkyard bell :
Ere yet the twelfth was silent quite,
    By him sat Isobel.

Within her arms their little child
    Lay pillowed on her breast :
Death seemed to it as soft and mild
    As heaven to the blest.

Ah, no more wasted was her face,
    Nor white her cheek and wan !
The splendor of a heavenly grace
    Upon her forehead shone.

She seemed again the golden girl
    Of the long-vanished years :
Her face shone as a great sweet pearl
    Washed and made white with tears.

The light of heaven filled her eyes
    With soft and splendid flame ;
Out of the heart of Paradise
    It seemed as if she came.

He looked upon her beauty bright ;
    And sore, sore weepit he,
To think how many a day and night
    Between them yet must be.

He looked at her with many a sigh ;
  For sick he was with pain,
To think how many a year must fly
  Ere they two met again.

She looked on him : no sadness lay
  Upon her tender mouth ;
Syne she smiled, a smile as gay
  And glad as in her youth.

' Be of good cheer, dear heart,' said she :
  ' Yet but a little year
Ere thou and I together see
  The end of doubt and fear.

' Come once again the saints' night ring
  Unto the spirits' feet,
Glad with the end of sorrowing,
  Once more we three shall meet :

' We three shall meet no more to part
  For all eternity ;
'Gin I come not to thee, sweetheart,
  Do thou come then to me.'

v.

Another year is past and gone :
  Once more the lingering light
Fades from the sky, and dusk falls down
  Upon the Holy Night.

The hearth is clear ; the fire burns red ;
  The door stands open wide :
He waits for the belovèd dead
  To come with Hallow-tide.

The midnight rings out loud and slow
  Across the frosty air :
He sits before the firelight glow,
  Beside the waiting chair.

The last chime dies into the night :
  The stillness grows apace :
And yet there comes no lady bright
  To fill the empty place.

No soft hand falls upon his hair :
  No light breath fans his brow :
The night is empty everywhere ;
  The birds sleep on the bough.

' Ah, woe is me ! the night fades fast :
  Her promise is forgot :
Alas ! ' he said, ' the hours fly past,
  And still she cometh not !

' So sweet she sleeps, and sleeps with her
  The baby at her breast,
No thought of earthly love can stir
  Their undesireful rest.

' Ah, who can tell but Time may lay
  Betwixt us such a space
That haply at the Judgment Day
  She will forget my face.'

The still night quivered as he spoke ;
  He felt the midnight air
Throb, and a little breeze awoke
  Across the heather bare.

And in the wind him seemed he heard
  His true love's voice once more:
Afar it came, and but one word
  'Come!' unto him it bore.

A faint hope flickered in his breast:
  He rose and took his way
Where underneath the brown hill's crest
  The quiet kirkyard lay.

He pushed the lychgate to the wall:
  Against the moonless sky
The grey kirk towered dusk and tall:
  Heaven seemed on it to lie.

Dead darkness held the holy ground;
  His feet went in and out,
And stumbled at each grassy mound,
  As one that is in doubt.

Then suddenly the sky grew white;
  The moon thrust through the gloom;
The tall tower's shade against her light
  Fell on his Minnie's tomb.

Full on her grave its shadow fell,
  As 't were a giant's hand,
That motionless the way doth tell
  Unto the heavenly land.

He fell upon his knees thereby
  And kissed the holy earth,
Wherein the only twain did lie
  That made life living-worth.

He knelt; no longer did he weep;
  Great peace was on his soul:
Sleep sank on him, a wondrous sleep,
  Assaining death and dole.

And in the sleep him seemed he stood
  Before a high gold door,
Upon whose midst the blessèd Rood
  Burnt like an opal's core.

Christ shining on the cross to see
  Was there for all device:
Within he saw the almond-tree
  That grows in Paradise.

He knew the fallen almond-flowers
  That drop without the gate,
So with their scent the tardy hours
  Be cheered for those that wait.

And as he looked, a glimmering light
  Shone through the blazoned bars.:
The wide tall gate grew blue and bright
  As Heaven with the stars.

A postern opened in his face;
  Sweet savors breathed about;
And through the little open space
  A fair white hand came out:

A hand as white as ermolin,
  A hand he knew full well,
Beckoned to him to enter in, —
  The hand of Isobel.

   .   .   .   .

Lord Christ, Thy morning tarrieth long :
  The shadows come and go :
These three have heard the angels' song :
  Still many wait below.

These three on Heaven's honey feed,
  And milk of Paradise :
How long before for us indeed
  The hills of Heaven rise ?

How long before, joined hand-in-hand
  With all the dear-loved dead,
We pass along the heavenly land
  And hear the angels' tread ?

The night is long : the way is drear :
  Our hearts faint for the light :
Vouchsafe, Lord Christ, the day draw near,
  The morning of Thy sight !

By Lord Tennyson.

THE FIRST QUARREL.

(IN THE ISLE OF WIGHT.)

'WAIT a little,' you say, 'you are sure it 'll all come right.'
But the boy was born i' trouble, an' looks so wan an' so
      white :
Wait ! an' once I ha' waited — I had n't to wait for long.
Now I wait, wait, wait for Harry. -- No, no, you are doing
      me wrong !
Harry and I were married : the boy can hold up his head.
The boy was born in wedlock, but after my man was dead :
I ha' worked for him fifteen years, an' I work an' I wait to
      the end.
I am all alone in the world, an' you are my only friend.

Doctor if *you* can wait, I 'll tell you the tale o' my life.
When Harry an' I were children, he called me his own
      little wife ;
I was happy when I was with him, an' sorry when he was
      away,
An' when we played together, I loved him better than
      play ;
He workt me the daisy chain — he made me the cowslip
      ball,
He fought the boys that were rude an' I loved him better
      than all.

Passionate girl tho' I was, an' often at home in disgrace,
I never could quarrel with Harry — I had but to look in
    his face.

There was a farmer in Dorset of Harry's kin, that had
    need
Of a good stout lad at his farm; he sent, an' the father
    agreed;
So Harry was bound to the Dorsetshire farm for years an'
    for years;
I walked with him down to the quay, poor lad, an' we
    parted in tears.
The boat was beginning to move, we heard them a-ringing
    the bell,
' I 'll never love any but you, God bless you, my own little
    Nell.'

I was a child, an' he was a child, an' he came to harm;
There was a girl, a hussy, that workt with him up at the
    farm,
One had deceived her an' left her alone with her sin an'
    her shame,
And so she was wicked with Harry; the girl was the most
    to blame.

And years went over till I that was little had grown so
    tall,
The men would say of the maids, ' Our Nelly 's the flower
    of 'em all.'
I did n't take heed o' *them*, but I taught myself all I
    could
To make a good wife for Harry, when Harry came home
    for good.

Often I seemed unhappy, and often as happy too,
For I heard it abroad in the fields, 'I 'll never love any but
     you;'
'I 'll never love any but you' the morning song of the
     lark,
'I 'll never love any but you' the nightingale's hymn in the
     dark.

And Harry came home at last, but he looked at me sidelong
     and shy,
Vext me a bit, till he told me that so many years had gone
     by,
I had grown so handsome and tall — that I might ha' forgot
     him somehow,
For he thought — there were other lads -- he was feared to
     look at me now.

Hard was the frost in the field, we were married o' Christ-
     mas day,
Married among the red berries, an' all as merry as May —
Those were the pleasant times, my house an' my man were
     my pride,
We seemed like ships i' the Channel a-sailing with wind
     an' tide.

But work was scant in the Isle, tho' he tried the villages
     round,
So Harry went over the Solent to see if work could be
     found ;
An' he wrote, 'I ha' six weeks' work, little wife, so far as
     I know;
I 'll come for an hour to-morrow, an' kiss you before I go.'

So I set to righting the house, for was n't he coming that
    day?
An' I hit on an old deal-box that was pushed in a corner
    away;
It was full of old odds an' ends, an' a letter along wi' the
    rest,
I had better ha' put my naked hand in a hornet's nest.

' Sweetheart '— this was the letter — this was the letter I
    read —
' You promised to find me work enar you, an' I wish I was
    dead —
Did n't you kiss me an' promise? you have n't done it, my
    lad,
An' I almost died o' your going away, an' I wish that I
    had.'

I too wish that I had — in the pleasant times that had
    past,
Before I quarrelled with Harry — *my* quarrel — the first an'
    the last.

For Harry came in, an' I flung him the letter that drove me
    wild,
An' he told it me all at once, as simple as any child,
' What can it matter, my lass, what I did wi' my single
    life?
I ha' been as true to you as ever a man to his wife;
An' *she* was n't one o' the worst.' ' Then,' I said, ' I 'm
    none o' the best.'
An' he smiled at me, ' Ain't you, my love? Come, come.
    little wife, let it rest!

The man is n't like the woman, no need to make such a
   stir.'
But he angered me all the more, an' I said, 'You were
   keeping with her,
When I was a-loving you all along an' the same as before.'
An' he did n't speak for a while, an' he angered me more
   and more.
Then he patted my hand in his gentle way, 'Let by-gones
   be ! '
'By-gones ! you kept yours hushed,' I said, 'when you
   married me !
By-gones ma' be come-agains; an' *she*— in her shame an'
   her sin —
You 'll have her to nurse my child, if I die o' my lying
   in !
You 'll make her its second mother ! I hate her — an' I
   hate you ! '
Ah, Harry, my man, you had better ha' beaten me black
   an' blue
Than ha' spoken as kind as you did, when I were so crazy
   wi' spite,
' Wait a little, my lass, I am sure it 'll all come right.'

An' he took three turns in the rain, an' I watched him, an'
   when he came in
I felt that my heart was hard, he was all wet thro' to the
   skin,
An' I never said 'off wi' the wet,' I never said 'on wi' the
   dry,'
So I knew my heart was hard, when he came to bid me
   good-by.

'You said that you hated me, Ellen, but that is n't true,
you know ;
I am going to leave you a bit — you 'll kiss me before I
go ? '

'Going! you 're going to her — kiss her — if you will,' I
said, —
I was near my time wi' the boy, I must ha' been light i' my
head, —
'I had sooner be cursed than kissed !' — I did n't know
well what I meant,
But I turned my face from *him,* an' he turned *his* face an'
he went.

And then he sent me a letter, ' I 've gotten my work to do;
You would n't kiss me, my lass, an' I never loved any but
you ;
I am sorry for all the quarrel an' sorry for what she wrote,
I ha' six weeks' work in Jersey an' go to-night by the
boat.'

An' the wind began to rise, an' I thought of him out at
sea,
An' I felt I had been to blame; he was always kind to me.
'Wait a little, my lass, I am sure it 'll all come right ' —
An' the boat went down that night — the boat went down
that night.

By Dante Gabriel Rossetti.

THE KING'S TRAGEDY.[4]

James I. of Scots — 20th February. 1437.

I Catherine am a Douglas born,
  A name to all Scots dear;
And Kate Barlass they 've called me now
  Through many a waning year.

This old arm 's withered now. 'T was once
  Most deft 'mong maidens all
To rein the steed, to wing the shaft,
  To smite the palm-play ball.

In hall adown the close-linked dance
  It has shone most white and fair;
It has been the rest for a true lord's head,
And many a sweet babe's nursing-bed,
  And the bar to a King's chambère.

Ay, lasses, draw round Kate Barlass,
  And hark with bated breath
How good King James, King Robert's son,
  Was foully done to death.

Through all the days of his gallant youth
  The princely James was pent,
By his friends at first and then by his foes,
  In long imprisonment.

For the elder Prince, the kingdom's heir,
   By treason's murderous brood
Was slain; and the father quaked for the child
   With the royal mortal blood.

I' the Bass Rock fort, by his father's care,
   Was his childhood's life assured;
And Henry the subtle Bolingbroke
Proud England's King, 'neath the southron yoke
   His youth for long years immured.

Yet in all things meet for a kingly man
   Himself did he approve;
And the nightingale through his prison-wall
   Taught him both lore and love.

For once, when the bird's song drew him close
   To the opened window-pane,
In her bowers beneath a lady stood,
A light of life to his sorrowful mood,
   Like a lily amid the rain.

And for her sake, to the sweet bird's note
   He framed a sweeter song, —
More sweet than ever a poet's heart
   Gave yet to the English tongue.

She was a lady of royal blood;
   And when, past sorrow and teen,
He stood where still through his crownless years
   His Scotish realm had been,
At Scone were the happy lovers crowned,
   A heart-wed King and Queen.

But the bird may fall from the bough of youth,
  And song be turned to moan,
And Love's storm-cloud be the shadow of Hate,
When the tempest-waves of a troubled State
  Are beating against a throne.

Yet well they loved; and the god of Love,
  Whom well the King had sung,
Might find on the earth no truer hearts
  His lowliest swains among.

From the days when first she rode abroad
  With Scotish maids in her train,
I Catherine Douglas won the trust
  Of my mistress sweet Queen Jane.

And oft she sighed, ' To be born a King ! '
  And oft along the way,
When she saw the homely lovers pass
  She has said, ' Alack the day ! '

Years waned, — the loving and toiling years :
  Till England's wrong renewed
Drove James, by outrage cast on his crown,
  To the open field of feud.

'T was when the King and his host were met
  At the leaguer of Roxbro' hold,
The Queen o' the sudden sought his camp
  With a tale of dread to be told.

And she showed him a secret letter writ
  That spoke of treasonous strife,
And how a band of his noblest lords
  Were sworn to take his life.

'And it may be here or it may be there,
  In the camp or the court,' she said :
'But for my sake come to your people's arms
  And guard your royal head.'

Quoth he, ''T is the fifteenth day of the siege,
  And the castle 's nigh to yield.'
'Oh, face your foes on your throne,' she cried,
  'And show the power you wield;
And under your Scotish people's love
  You shall sit as under your shield.'

At the fair Queen's side I stood that day
  When he bade them raise the siege,
And back to his Court he sped to know
  How the lords would meet their Liege.

But when he summoned his Parliament,
  The louring brows hung round,
Like clouds that circle the mountain-head
  Ere the first low thunders sound.

For he had tamed the nobles' lust
  And curbed their power and pride,
And reached out an arm to right the poor
  Through Scotland far and wide ;
And many a lordly wrong-doer
  By the headsman's axe had died.

'T was then upspoke Sir Robert Græme,
  The bold o'ermastering man :
'O King, in the name of your Three Estates
  I set you under their ban !

'For, as your lords made oath to you
    Of service and fealty,
Even in like wise you pledged your oath
    Their faithful sire to be;

' Yet all we here that are nobly sprung
    Have mourned dear kith and kin
Since first for the Scotish Barons' curse
    Did your bloody rule begin.'

With that he laid his hands on his King:
    'Is this not so, my lords?'
But of all who had sworn to league with him
    Not one spake back to his words.

Quoth the King: 'Thou speak'st but for one Estate,
    Nor doth it avow thy gage.
Let my liege lords hale this traitor hence!'
    The Græme fired dark with rage:
'Who works for lesser men than himself,
    He earns but a witless wage!'

But soon from the dungeon where he lay
    He won by privy plots,
And forth he fled with a price on his head
    To the country of the Wild Scots.

And word there came from Sir Robert Græme
    To the King at Edinbro':
'No Liege of mine thou art; but I see
From this day forth alone in thee
    God's creature, my mortal foe.

'Through thee are my wife and children lost,
  My heritage and lands ;
And when my God shall show me a way,
Thyself my mortal foe will I slay
  With these my proper hands.'

Against the coming of Christmastide
  That year the King bade call
I' the Black Friars' Charterhouse of Perth
  A solemn festival.

And we of his household rode with him
  In a close-ranked company ;
But not till the sun had sunk from his throne
  Did we reach the Scotish Sea.

That eve was clenched for a boding storm,
  'Neath a toilsome moon half seen ;
The cloud stooped low and the surf rose high ;
And where there was a line of the sky,
  Wild wings loomed dark between.

And on a rock of the black beach-side,
  By the veiled moon dimly lit,
There was something seemed to heave with life
  As the King drew nigh to it.

And was it only the tossing furze
  Or break of the waste sea-wold ?
Or was it an eagle bent to the blast ?
When near we came, we knew it at last
  For a woman tattered and old.

But it seemed as though by a fire within
  Her writhen limbs were wrung;
And as soon as the King was close to her,
  She stood up gaunt and strong.

'T was then the moon sailed clear of the rack
  On high in her hollow dome;
And still as aloft with hoary crest
  Each clamorous wave rang home,
Like fire in snow the moonlight blazed
  Amid the champing foam.

And the woman held his eyes with her eyes:
  'O King, thou art come at last;
But thy wraith has haunted the Scotish Sea
  To my sight for four years past.

'Four years it is since first I met,
  'Twixt the Duchray and the Dhu,
A shape whose feet clung close in a shroud,
  And that shape for thine I knew.

'A year again, and on Inchkeith Isle
  I saw thee pass in the breeze,
With the cerecloth risen above thy feet
  And wound about thy knees.

'And yet a year, in the Links of Forth,
  As a wanderer without rest,
Thou cam'st with both thine arms i' the shroud
  That clung high up thy breast.

'And in this hour I find thee here,
  And well mine eyes may note
That the winding-sheet hath passed thy breast
  And risen around thy throat.

'And when I meet thee again, O King,
  That of death hast such sore drouth, —
Except thou turn again on this shore, —
The winding-sheet shall have moved once more
  And covered thine eyes and mouth.

'O King, whom poor men bless for their King,
  Of thy fate be not so fain ;
But these my words for God's message take,
And turn thy steed, O King, for her sake
  Who rides beside thy rein !'

While the woman spoke, the King's horse reared
  As if it would breast the sea ;
And the Queen turned pale as she heard on the gale
  The voice die dolorously.

When the woman ceased, the steed was still,
  But the King gazed on her yet,
And in silence save for the wail of the sea
  His eyes and her eyes met.

At last he said : 'God's ways are His own ;
  Man is but shadow and dust.
Last night I prayed by His altar-stone ;
To-night I wend to the Feast of His Son ;
  And in Him I set my trust.

' I have held my people in sacred charge,
   And have not feared the sting
Of proud men's hate, — to His will resigned
   Who has but one same death for a hind
   And one same death for a King.

'And if God in His wisdom have brought close
   The day when I must die,
That day by water or fire or air
   My feet shall fall in the destined snare
   Wherever my road may lie.

' What man can say but the Fiend hath set
   Thy sorcery on my path,
My heart with the fear of death to fill,
And turn me against God's very will
   To sink in His burning wrath ? '

The woman stood as the train rode past,
   And moved nor limb nor eye ;
And when we were shipped, we saw her there
   Still standing against the sky.

As the ship made way, the moon once more
   Sank slow in her rising pall ;
And I thought of the shrouded wraith of the King,
   And I said, ' The Heavens know all.'

And now, ye lasses, must ye hear
   How my name is Kate Barlass, —
But a little thing, when all the tale
   Is told of the weary mass
Of crime and woe which in Scotland's realm
   God's will let come to pass.

'T was in the Charterhouse of Perth
    That the King and all his Court
Were met, the Christmas Feast being done,
    For solace and disport.

'T was a wind-wild eve in February,
    And against the casement-pane
The branches smote like summoning hands,
    And muttered the driving rain.

And when the wind swooped over the lift
    And made the whole heaven frown,
It seemed a grip was laid on the walls
    To tug the house-top down.

And the Queen was there, more stately fair
    Than a lily in garden set ;
And the King was loth to stir from her side ;
For as on the day when she was his bride,
    Even so he loved her yet.

And the Earl of Athole, the King's false friend,
    Sat with him at the board ;
And Robert Stuart the chamberlain
    Who had sold his sovereign Lord.

Yet the traitor Christopher Chaumber there
    Would fain have told him all,
And vainly four times that night he strove
    To reach the King through the hall.

But the wine is bright at the goblet's brim
    Though the poison lurk beneath ;
And the apples still are red on the tree
Within whose shade may the adder be
    That shall turn thy life to death.

There was a knight of the King's fast friends
    Whom he called the King of Love;
And to such bright cheer and courtesy
    That name might best behove.

And the King and Queen both loved him well
    For his gentle knightliness;
And with him the King, as that eve wore on,
    Was playing at the chess.

And the King said (for he thought to jest
    And soothe the Queen thereby):
'In a book 't is writ that this same year
    A King shall in Scotland die.

'And I have pondered the matter o'er,
    And this I have found, Sir Hugh, —
There are but two Kings on Scotish ground,
    And those Kings are I and you.

'And I have a wife and a new-born heir,
    And you are yourself alone;
So stand you stark at my side with me
    To guard our double throne.

'For here sit I and my wife and child,
    As well your heart shall approve,
In full surrender and soothfastness,
    Beneath your Kingdom of Love.'

And the Knight laughed, and the Queen too smiled;
    But I knew her heavy thought,
And I strove to find in the good King's jest
    What cheer might thence be wrought.

And I said, 'My Liege, for the Queen's dear love
  Now sing the song that of old
You made, when a captive Prince you lay,
And the nightingale sang sweet on the spray,
  In Windsor's castle-hold.'

Then he smiled the smile I knew so well
  When he thought to please the Queen,
The smile which under all bitter frowns
  Of hate that rose between
Forever dwelt at the poet's heart
  Like the bird of love unseen.

And he kissed her hand and took his harp,
  And the music sweetly rang ;
And when the song burst forth, it seemed
  'T was the nightingale that sang.

' *Worship, ye lovers, on this May :*
  Of bliss your kalends are begun :
Sing with us, Away, Winter, away !
  Come, Summer, the sweet season and sun !
  Awake for shame, — your heaven is won, —
And amorously your heads lift all :
Thank Love, that you to his grace doth call ! '

But when he bent to the Queen, and sang
  The speech whose praise was hers,
It seemed his voice was the voice of the Spring
  And the voice of the by-gone years.

' *The fairest and the freshest flower*
That ever I saw before that hour,

The which o' the sudden made to start
The blood of my body to my heart.

. . . .

Ah sweet, are ye a worldly creature,
Or heavenly thing in form of nature ?'

And the song was long, and richly stored
    With wonder and beauteous things ;
And the harp was tuned to every change
    Of minstrel ministerings ;
But when he spoke of the Queen at the last,
    Its strings were his own heart-strings.

' *Unworthy but only of her grace,*
    Upon Love's rock that's easy and sure,
In guerdon of all my love's space
    She took me her humble creäture.
    Thus fell my blissful aventure
In youth of love that from day to day
Flowereth aye new, and further I say.

' *To reckon all the circumstance*
    As it happed when lessen gan my sore,
Of my rancor and woful chance,
    It were too long, — I have done therefor,
    And of this flower I say no more
But unto my help her heart hath tended
And even from death her man defended.'

' Aye, even from death,' to myself I said ;
    For I thought of the day when she
Had borne him the news, at Roxbro' siege,
    Of the fell confederacy.

But Death even then took aim as he sang
   With an arrow deadly bright ;
And the grinning skull lurked grimly aloof,
And the wings were spread far over the roof
   More dark than the winter night.

Yet truly along the amorous song
   Of Love's high pomp and state
There were words of Fortune's trackless doom.
   And the dreadful face of Fate.

And oft have I heard again in dreams
   The voice of dire appeal
In which the King then sang of the pit
   That is under Fortune's wheel.

' *And under the wheel beheld I there*
   An ugly Pit as deep as hell,
That to behold I quaked for fear :
   And this I heard, that who therein fell
   Came no more up, tidings to tell :
Whereat, astound of the fearful sight,
I wist not what to do for fright.'

And oft has my thought called up again
   These words of the changeful song :
' *Wist thou thy pain and thy travàil*
To come, well might'st thou weep and wail ! '
   And our wail, O God ! is long.

But the song's end was all of his love ;
   And well his heart was graced
With her smiling lips and her tear-bright eyes
   As his arm went round her waist.

And on the swell of her long fair throat
  Close clung the necklet-chain
As he bent her pearl-tired head aside,
And in the warmth of his love and pride
  He kissed her lips full fain.

And her true face was a rosy red,
  The very red of the rose
That, couched on the happy garden-bed,
  In the summer sunlight glows.

And all the wondrous things of love
  That sang so sweet through the song
Were in the look that met in their eyes,
  And the look was deep and long.

'T was then a knock came at the outer gate,
  And the usher sought the King.
' The woman you met by the Scotish Sea,
  My Liege, would tell you a thing ;
And she says that her present need for speech
  Will bear no gainsaying.'

And the King said : ' The hour is late ;
  To-morrow will serve, I ween.'
Then he charged the usher strictly, and said :
  ' No word of this to the Queen.'

But the usher came again to the King.
  ' Shall I call her back ? ' quoth he :
' For as she went on her way, she cried,
  " Woe ! Woe ! then the thing must be ! " '

And the King paused, but he did not speak.
  Then he called for the Voidee-cup:
And as we heard the twelfth hour strike,
There by true lips and false lips alike
  Was the draught of trust drained up.

So with reverence meet to King and Queen
  To bed went all from the board;
And the last to leave of the courtly train
Was Robert Stuart the chamberlain
  Who had sold his sovereign lord.

And all the locks of the chamber-door
  Had the traitor riven and brast;
And that Fate might win sure way from afar,
He had drawn out every bolt and bar
  That made the entrance fast.

And now at midnight he stole his way
  To the moat of the outer wall,
And laid strong hurdles closely across
  Where the traitors' tread should fall.

But we that were the Queen's bower-maids
  Alone were left behind;
And with heed we drew the curtains close
  Against the winter wind.

And now that all was still through the hall,
  More clearly we heard the rain
That clamored ever against the glass,
  And the boughs that beat on the pane.

But the fire was bright in the ingle-nook,
   And through empty space around
The shadows cast on the arrased wall
'Mid the pictured kings stood sudden and tall
   Like spectres sprung from the ground.

And the bed was dight in a deep alcove;
   And as he stood by the fire
The King was still in talk with the Queen
   While he doffed his goodly attire.

And the song had brought the image back
   Of many a by-gone year;
And many a loving word they said
With hand in hand and head laid to head;
   And none of us went anear.

But Love was weeping outside the house,
   A child in the piteous rain;
And as he watched the arrow of Death,
He wailed for his own shafts close in the sheath
   That never should fly again.

And now beneath the window arose
   A wild voice suddenly:
And the King reared straight, but the Queen fell back
   As for bitter dule to dree;
And all of us knew the woman's voice
   Who spoke by the Scotish Sea.

' O King,' she cried, ' in an evil hour
   They drove me from thy gate;
And yet my voice must rise to thine ears;
   But alas! it comes too late!

' Last night at mid-watch, by Aberdour,
    When the moon was dead in the skies,
O King, in a death-light of thine own
    I saw thy shape arise.

' And in full season, as erst I said,
    The doom had gained its growth ;
And the shroud had risen above thy neck
    And covered thine eyes and mouth.

' And no moon woke, but the pale dawn broke,
    And still thy soul stood there ;
And I thought its silence cried to my soul
    As the first rays crowned its hair.

' Since then have I journeyed fast and fain
    In very despite of Fate,
Lest Hope might still be found in God's will :
    But they drove me from thy gate.

' For every man on God's ground, O King,
    His death grows up from his birth
In a shadow-plant perpetually ;
And thine towers high, a black yew-tree,
    O'er the Charterhouse of Perth ! '

That room was built far out from the house;
    And none but we in the room
Might hear the voice that rose beneath,
    Nor the tread of the coming doom.

For now there came a torchlight-glare,
    And a clang of arms there came ;
And not a soul in that space but thought
    Of the foe Sir Robert Græme.

Yea, from the country of the Wild Scots,
  O'er mountain, valley, and glen,
He had brought with him in murderous league
  Three hundred armèd men.

The King knew all in an instant's flash,
  And like a King did he stand ;
But there was no armor in all the room,
  Nor weapon lay to his hand.

And all we women flew to the door
  And thought to have made it fast ;
But the bolts were gone and the bars were gone
  And the locks were riven and brast.

And he caught the pale, pale Queen in his arms
  As the iron footsteps fell, —
Then loosed her, standing alone, and said,
  ' Our bliss was our farewell ! '

And 'twixt his lips he murmured a prayer,
  And he crossed his brow and breast ;
And proudly in royal hardihood
Even so with folded arms he stood, —
  The prize of the bloody quest.

Then on me leaped the Queen like a deer.
  ' O Catherine, help ! ' she cried.
And low at his feet we clasped his knees
  Together side by side.
' Oh ! even a King, for his people's sake,
  From treasonous death must hide ! '

' For *her* sake most ! ' I cried, and I marked
  The pang that my words could wring.
And the iron tongs from the chimney-nook
  I snatched and held to the King :
' Wrench up the plank ! and the vault beneath
  Shall yield safe harboring.'

With brows low-bent, from my eager hand
  The heavy heft did he take ;
And the plank at his feet he wrenched and tore ;
And as he frowned through the open floor,
  Again I said, ' For her sake ! '

Then he cried to the Queen, ' God's will be done ! '
  For her hands were clasped in prayer.
And down he sprang to the inner crypt ;
And straight we closed the plank he had ripped
  And toiled to smooth it fair.

(Alas ! in that vault a gap once was
  Wherethro' the King might have fled :
But three days since close-walled had it been
By his will ; for the ball would roll therein
  When without at the palm he played.)

Then the Queen cried, ' Catherine, keep the door,
  And I to this will suffice ! '
At her word I rose all dazed to my feet,
  And my heart was fire and ice.

And louder ever the voices grew,
  And the tramp of men in mail ;
Until to my brain it seemed to be
As though I tossed on a ship at sea
  In the teeth of a crashing gale.

Then back I flew to the rest; and hard
    We strove with sinews knit
To force the table against the door;
    But we might not compass it.

Then my wild gaze sped far down the hall
    To the place of the hearthstone-sill;
And the Queen bent ever above the floor,
    For the plank was rising still.

And now the rush was heard on the stair,
    And 'God, what help?' was our cry.
And was I frenzied or was I bold?
I looked at each empty stanchion-hold,
    And no bar but my arm had I!

Like iron felt my arm, as through
    The staple I made it pass:
Alack! it was flesh and bone — no more!
'T was Catherine Douglas sprang to the door,
    But I fell back Kate Barlass.

With that they all thronged into the hall,
    Half dim to my failing ken;
And the space that was but a void before
    Was a crowd of wrathful men.

Behind the door I had fall'n and lay,
    Yet my sense was wildly aware,
And for all the pain of my shattered arm
    I never fainted there.

Even as I fell, my eyes were cast
    Where the King leaped down to the pit;
And lo! the plank was smooth in its place,
    And the Queen stood far from it.

And under the litters and through the bed
  And within the presses all
The traitors sought for the King, and pierced
  The arras around the wall.

And through the chamber they ramped and stormed
  Like lions loose in the lair,
And scarce could trust to their very eyes, —
  For behold! no King was there.

Then one of them seized the Queen, and cried,
  ' Now tell us, where is thy lord ?'
And he held the sharp point over her heart :
She drooped not her eyes nor did she start,
  But she answered never a word.

Then the sword half pierced the true, true breast :
  But it was the Græme's own son
Cried, ' This is a woman, — we seek a man !'
  And away from her girdle-zone
He struck the point of the murderous steel ;
  And that foul deed was not done.

And forth flowed all the throng like a sea,
  And 't was empty space once more ;
And my eyes sought out the wounded Queen
  As I lay behind the door.

And I said : ' Dear lady, leave me here,
  For I cannot help you now ;
But fly while you may, and none shall reck
  Of my place here lying low.'

And she said, 'My Catherine, God help thee ! '
    Then she looked to the distant floor,
And clasping her hands, ' O God help *him*,'
    She sobbed, ' for we can no more ! '

But God He knows what help may mean,
    If it mean to live or to die ;
And what sore sorrow and mighty moan
On earth it may cost ere yet a throne
    Be filled in His house on high.

And now the ladies fled with the Queen :
    And thorough the open door
The night-wind wailed round the empty room
    And the rushes shook on the floor.

And the bed drooped low in the dark recess
    Whence the arras was rent away ;
And the firelight still shone over the space
    Where our hidden secret lay.

And the rain had ceased, and the moonbeams lit
    The window high in the wall, —
Bright beams that on the plank that I knew
    Through the painted pane did fall,
And gleamed with the splendor of Scotland's crown
    And shield armorial.

But then a great wind swept up the skies,
    And the climbing moon fell back ;
And the royal blazon fled from the floor,
    And nought remained on its track ;
And high in the darkened window-pane
    The shield and the crown were black.

And what I say next I partly saw
  And partly I heard, in sooth,
And partly since from the murderers' lips
  The torture wrung the truth.

For now again came the armèd tread,
  And fast through the hall it fell;
But the throng was less: and ere I saw,
  By the voice without I could tell
That Robert Stuart had come with them,
  Who knew that chamber well.

And over the space the Græme strode dark
  With his mantle round him flung;
And in his eye was a flaming light,
  But not a word on his tongue.

And Stuart held a torch to the floor,
  And he found the thing he sought;
And they slashed the plank away with their swords:
  And, O God! I fainted not!

And the traitor held his torch in the gap,
  All smoking and smouldering;
And through the vapor and fire, beneath
  In the dark crypt's narrow ring,
With a shout that pealed to the room's high roof
  They saw their naked King.

Half naked he stood, but stood as one
  Who yet could do and dare:
With the crown, the King was stript away, —
The Knight was reft of his battle-array, —
  But still the Man was there.

From the rout then stepped a villain forth, —
  Sir John Hall was his name;
With a knife unsheathed he leaped to the vault
  Beneath the torchlight-flame.

Of his person and stature was the King
  A man right manly strong,
And mightily by the shoulder-blades
  His foe to his feet he flung.

Then the traitor's brother, Sir Thomas. Hall,
  Sprang down to work his worst;
And the King caught the second man by the neck
  And flung him above the first.

And he smote and trampled them under him;
  And a long month thence they bare
All black their throats with the grip of his hands
  When the hangman's hand came there.

And sore he strove to have had their knives,
  But the sharp blades gashed his hands.
O James! so armed, thou hadst battled there
  Till help had come of thy bands;
And oh! once more thou hadst held our throne
  And ruled thy Scotish lands!

But while the King o'er his foes still raged
  With a heart that nought could tame,
Another man sprang down to the crypt;
And with his sword in his hand hard-gripped,
  There stood Sir Robert Græme.

(Now shame on the recreant traitor's heart
  Who durst not face his King
Till the body unarmed was wearied out
  With twofold combating!

Ah! well might the people sing and say,
  As oft ye have heard aright:
'*O Robert Græme, O Robert Græme,*
Who slew our King, God give thee shame!'
  For he slew him not as a knight.)

And the naked King turned round at bay,
  But his strength had passed the goal,
And he could but gasp: 'Mine hour is come;
But oh, to succor thine own soul's doom,
  Let a priest now shrive my soul!'

And the traitor looked on the King's spent strength
  And said: 'Have I kept my word? —
Yea, King, the mortal pledge that I gave?
No black friar's shrift thy soul shall have,
  But the shrift of this red sword!'

With that he smote his King through the breast;
  And all they three in that pen
Fell on him and stabbed and stabbed him there
  Like merciless murderous men.

Yet seemed it now that Sir Robert Græme,
  Ere the King's last breath was o'er,
Turned sick at heart with the deadly sight,
  And would have done no more.

But a cry came from the troop above :
　‘ If him thou do not slay,
The price of his life that thou dost spare
　Thy forfeit life shall pay !’

O God ! what more did I hear or see,
　Or how should I tell the rest ?
But there at length our King lay slain
　With sixteen wounds in his breast.

O God ! and now did a bell boom forth,
　And the murderers turned and fled ; —
Too late, too late, O God, did it sound ! —
And I heard the true men mustering round,
　And the cries and the coming tread.

But ere they came, to the black death-gap
　Somewise did I creep and steal ;
And lo ! or ever I swooned away,
Through the dusk I saw where the white face lay
　In the Pit of Fortune’s Wheel.

And now, ye Scotish maids who have heard
　Dread things of the days grown old, —
Even at the last, of true Queen Jane
　May somewhat yet be told,
And how she dealt for her dear lord’s sake
　Dire vengeance manifold.

’T was in the Charterhouse of Perth,
　In the fair-lit Death-chapelle,
That the slain King’s corpse on bier was laid
　With chaunt and requiem-knell.

And all with royal wealth of balm
    Was the body purified;
And none could trace on the brow and lips
    The death that he had died.

In his robes of state he lay asleep
    With orb and sceptre in hand ;
And by the crown he wore on his throne
    Was his kingly forehead spanned.

And, girls, 't was a sweet sad thing to see
    How the curling golden hair,
As in the day of the poet's youth,
    From the King's crown clustered there.

And if all had come to pass in the brain
    That throbbed beneath those curls,
Then Scots had said in the days to come
That this their soil was a different home
    And a different Scotland, girls!

And the Queen sat by him night and day,
    And oft she knelt in prayer,
All wan and pale in the widow's veil
    That shrouded her shining hair.

And I had got good help of my hurt;
    And only to me some sign
She made; and save the priests that were there,
    No face would she see but mine.

And the month of March wore on apace ;
    And now fresh couriers fared
Still from the country of the Wild Scots
    With news of the traitors snared.

And still as I told her day by day,
  Her pallor changed to sight,
And the frost grew to a furnace-flame
  That burnt her visage white.

And evermore as I brought her word,
  She bent to her dead King James,
And in the cold ear with fire-drawn breath
  She spoke the traitors' names.

But when the name of Sir Robert Græme
  Was the one she had to give,
I ran to hold her up from the floor;
For the froth was on her lips, and sore
  I feared that she could not live.

And the month of March wore nigh to its end,
  And still was the death-pall spread;
For she would not bury her slaughtered lord
  Till his slayers all were dead.

And now of their dooms dread tidings came,
  And of torments fierce and dire;
And nought she spake, — she had ceased to speak, —
  But her eyes were a soul on fire.

But when I told her the bitter end
  Of the stern and just award,
She leaned o'er the bier, and thrice three times
  She kissed the lips of her lord.

And then she said,   'My King, they are dead!'
  And she knelt on the chapel-floor,
And whispered low with a strange proud smile,
  'James, James, they suffered more!'

Last she stood up to her queenly height,
  But she shook like an autumn leaf,
As though the fire wherein she burned
Then left her body, and all were turned
  To winter of life-long grief.

And ' O James !' she said, — 'My James !' she said, —
  ' Alas for the woful thing,
That a poet true and a friend of man,
In desperate days of bale and ban,
  Should needs be born a King !'

By Hamilton Aïdè.

LOST AND FOUND.

SOME miners were sinking a shaft in Wales
(I know not where,—but the facts have filled
A chink in my brain, while other tales

Have been swept away, as when pearls are spilled,
One pearl rolls into a chink in the floor;)
—Somewhere, then, where God's light is killed,

And men tear in the dark at the earth's heart-core.
These men were at work, when their axes knocked
A hole in a passage closed years before.

A slip in the earth, I suppose, had blocked
This gallery suddenly up, with a heap
Of rubble, as safe as a chest is locked,

Till these men picked it, and 'gan to creep
In on all-fours; then a loud shout ran
Round the black roof, ' Here 's a man asleep!'

They all pushed forward, and scarce a span
From the mouth of the passage, in sooth, the lamp
Fell on the upturned face of a man.

No taint of death, no decaying damp
Had touched that fair young brow, whereon
Courage had set its glorious stamp.

Lost and Found.

Calm as a monarch upon his throne,
Lips hard clenched, no shadow of fear,
He sat there taking his rest, alone.

He must have been there for many a year.
The spirit had fled; but there was its shrine,
In clothes of a century old or near!

The dry and embalming air of the mine
Had arrested the natural hand of decay,
Nor faded the flesh, nor dimmed a line.

Who was he, then? No man could say
When the passage had suddenly fallen in —
Its memory, even, was passed away!

Awe-struck they stood: then touched the skin,
And handled the cloth. The flame o' the soul
Had been blown out, ere its lamp grew thin.

In their great rough arms, begrimed with coal, .
They took him up, as a tender lass
Will carry a babe, from that darksome hole,

To the outer world of the short warm grass.
Then up spoke one, 'Let us send for Bess,
She is seventy-nine, come Martinmas;

'Older than any one here, I guess!
Belike, she may mind when the wall fell there,
And remember the chap by his comeliness.'

So they brought old Bess with her silver hair
To the side of the hill, where the dead man lay,
Ere the flesh had crumbled in outer air.

And the crowd around them all gave way,
As with tottering steps old Bess drew nigh,
And bent o'er the face of the unchanged clay.

Then suddenly rang a sharp low cry! . . .
Bess sank on her knees, and wildly tossed
Her withered arms in the summer sky . . .

'O Willie! Willie! my lad! my lost!
The Lord be praised! after sixty years,
I see you again! . . . The tears you cost,

'O Willie darlin', were bitter tears! . . .
They never looked for ye underground,
They told me a tale to mock my fears!

'They said ye were auver the sea, — ye'd found
A lass ye loved better nor me, to explain
How ye'd a vanished fra sight and sound!

'O darlin', a long, long life o' pain
I ha' lived since then! . . . And now I'm old,
'Seems a'most as if youth were come back again,

'Seeing ye there wi' your locks o' gold,
And limbs as straight as ashen beams, . . .
I a'most forget how the years ha' rolled

'Between us! . . . O Willie! how strange it seems
To see ye here as I've seen ye oft, . . .
Auver and auver again in dreams!'

In broken words like these, with soft
Low wails she rocked herself.   And none
Of the rough men around her scoffed.

For surely a sight like this the sun
Had rarely looked upon.   Face to face,
The old dead love and the living one !

The dead, with its undimmed fleshly grace,
At the end of threescore years; the quick,
Puckered and withered, without a trace

Of its warm girl-beauty !   A wizard's trick
Bringing the youth and the love that were,
Back to the eyes of the old and sick !

Those bodies were just of one age ; yet there
Death, clad in youth, had been standing still,
While Life had been fretting itself threadbare !

But the moment was come — (as a moment will
To all who have loved, and have parted here,
And have toiled alone up the thorny hill;

When, at the top, as their eyes see clear,
Over the mists in the vale below,
Mere specks their trials and toils appear,

Beside the eternal rest they know !)
Death came to old Bess that night, and gave
The welcome summons that she should go.

And now, though the rains and winds may rave,
Nothing can part them.   Deep and wide,
The miners that evening dug one grave.

And there, while the summers and winters glide.
Old Bess and young Willie sleep side by side !

By Lewis Morris.

AZENOR.

'SEAMEN, seamen, tell me true,
Is there any of your crew
Who in Armor Town has seen
Azenor, the kneeling queen?'

'We have seen her oft indeed,
Kneeling in the self-same place;
Brave her heart, though pale her face,
White her soul, though dark her weed.'

I.

Of a long-past summer day,
Envoys came from far away,
Mailed in silver, clothed with gold,
On their snorting chargers bold.

When the warder spied them near,
To the King he went, and cried,
'Twelve bold knights come pricking here:
Shall I open to them wide?'

'Let the great gates opened be,
See the knights are welcomed all;
Spread the board and deck the hall;
We will feast them royally.'

'By our Prince's high command,
Who one day shall be our King,
We come to ask a precious thing, —
Azenor your daughter's hand.'

'Gladly we will grant your prayer:
Brave the youth, as we have heard.
Tall is she, milk-white and fair,
Gentle as a singing bird.'

Fourteen days high feast they made,
Fourteen days of dance and song;
Till the dawn the harpers played;
Mirth and joyance all day long.

'Now, my fair spouse, it is meet
That we turn us toward our home.'
'As you will, my love, my sweet;
Where you are, there I would come.'

II.

When his step-dame saw the bride,
Well-nigh choked with spleen was she:
'This pale-faced girl, this lump of pride —
And shall she be preferred to me?

'New things please men best, 't is true,
And the old are cast aside.
Natheless, what is old and tried
Serves far better than the new.'

Scarce eight months had passed away,
When she to the Prince would come,

And with subtlety would say,
'Would you lose both wife and home?

'Have a care lest what I tell
Should befall you; so 't were best
Have a care and guard you well,
'Ware the cuckoo in your nest.'

'Madam, if the truth you tell,
Meet reward her crime shall earn,
First the round tower's straitest cell,
Then in nine days she shall burn.'

III.

When the old King was aware,
Bitter tears the greybeard shed.
Tore in grief his white, white hair,
Crying, 'Would God that I were dead!'

And to all the seamen said,
'Good seamen, pray you tell me true,
Is there, then, any one of you
Can tell me if my child be dead?'

'My liege, as yet alive is she,
Though burned to-morrow shall she be;
But from her prison tower, O King!
Morning and eve we hear her sing.

'Morning and eve, from her fair throat
Issues the same plaintive note,
"They are deceived; I kiss Thy rod:
Have pity on them, O my God!"'

IV.

Even as a lamb who gives its life
All meekly to the cruel knife,
White-robed she went, her soft feet bare,
Self-shrouded in her golden hair.

And as she to her dreadful fate
Fared on, poor innocent, meek and mild,
' Grave crime it were,' cried small and great,
' To slay the mother and the child.'

All wept sore, both small and great ;
Only the step-dame smiling sate :
' Sure 't were no evil deed, but good,
To kill the viper with her brood.'

' Quick, good fireman, fan the fire
Till it leap forth fierce and red ;
Fan it fierce as my desire :
She shall burn till she is dead.'

Vain their efforts, — all in vain,
Though they fanned and fanned again ;
The more they blew, the embers gray
Faded and sank and died away.

When the judge the portent saw,
Dazed and sick with fear was he :
' She is a witch, she flouts the law ;
Come, let us drown her in the sea.'

v.

What saw you on the sea?   A boat
Neither by sail nor oarsman sped;
And at the helm, to watch it float,
An angel white with wings outspread;

A little boat, far out to sea,
And with her child a fair ladye,
Whom at her breast she sheltered well,
Like a white dove upon a shell.

She kissed, and clasped, and kissed again
His little back, his little feet,
Crooning a soft and tender strain,
' Da-da, my dear; da-da, my sweet.

' Ah, could your father see you, sweet,
A proud man should he be to-day;
But we on earth may never meet,
But he is lost and far away.'

vi.

In Armor Town is such affright
As never castle knew before,
For at the midmost hour of night
The wicked step-dame is no more.

' I see hell open at my side:
Oh, save me, in God's name, my son!
Your spouse was chaste; 't was I who lied;
Oh, save me, for I am undone!'

Scarce had she checked her lying tongue,
When from her lips a snake did glide,
With threatening jaws which hissed and stung,
And pierced her marrow till she died.

Eftsoons, to foreign realms the knight
Went forth, by land and over sea;
Seeking in vain his lost delight,
O'er all the round, round world went he.

He sought her East, he sought her West,
Next to the hot South sped he forth,
Then, after many a fruitless quest,
He sought her in the gusty North.

There, by some nameless island vast,
His anchor o'er the side he cast;
When by a brooklet's fairy spray
He spies a little lad at play.

Fair are his locks, and blue his eyes
As his lost love's or as the sea;
The good knight, looking on them, sighs,
' Fair child, who may thy father be?'

' Sir, I have none save Him in heaven;
Long years ago he went away,
Ere I was born, and I am seven;
My mother mourns him night and day.'

' Who is thy mother, child, and where?'
' She cleanses linen, white and fair,
In yon clear stream.' ' Come, child, and we
Together will thy mother see.'

He took the youngling by the hand,
And, as they passed the yellow strand,
The child's swift blood in pulse and arm
Leapt to his father's and grew warm.

' Rise up and look, O mother dear;
It is my father who is here;
My father who was lost is come —
Oh, bless God for it ! — to his home.'

They knelt and blessed His holy name,
Who is so good, and just, and mild,
Who joins the sire and wife and child:
And so to Brittany they came.

And may the blessed Trinity
Protect all toilers of the sea !

By Sidney Lanier.

THE REVENGE OF HAMISH.

IT was three slim does and a ten-tined buck in the bracken
  lay;
  And all of a sudden the sinister smell of a man,
  Awaft on a wind-shift, wavered and ran
Down the hillside, and sifted along through the bracken
  and passed that way.

Then Nan got a-tremble at nostril; she was the daintiest
  doe;
  In the print of her velvet flank on the velvet fern
  She reared, and rounded her ears in turn.
Then the buck leapt up, and his head as a king's to a
  crown did go

Full high in the breeze, and he stood as if Death had the
  form of a deer;
  And the two slim does long lazily stretching arose,
  For their day-dream slowlier came to a close,
Till they woke and were still, breath-bound with waiting
  and wonder and fear.

Then Alan the huntsman sprang over the hillock, the
  hounds shot by,
  The does and the ten-tined buck made a marvellous
  bound,

The hounds swept after with never a sound,
But Alan loud winded his horn in sign that the quarry was
    nigh.

For at dawn of that day proud Maclean of Lockbury to the
    hunt had waxed wild,
    And he cursed at old Alan till Alan fared off with the
        hounds
    For to drive him the deer to the lower glen-grounds:
' I will kill a red deer,' quoth Maclean, ' in sight of the wife
    and child.'

So gayly he paced with his wife and the child to his chosen
    stand;
    But he hurried tall Hamish the henchman ahead : ' Go
        turn,' —
    Cried Maclean — ' if the deer seek to cross the burn,
Do thou turn them to me : nor fail, lest thy back be red as
    thy hand.'

Now hard-fortuned Hamish, half-blown of his breath with
    the height of the hill,
    Was white in the face when the ten-tined buck and the
        does
    Drew leaping to burn-ward; huskily rose
His shouts, and his nether lip twitched, and his legs were
    o'er-weak for his will.

So the deer darted lightly by Hamish, and bounded away
    to the burn.
    But Maclean, never bating his watch, tarried waiting
    below.

Still Hamish hung heavy with fear for to go
All the space of an hour; then he went, and his face was
    greenish and stern,

And his eye sat back in the socket, and shrunken the eye-
    balls shone,
  As withdrawn from a vision of deeds it were shame to see.
  'Now, now, grim henchman, what is 't with thee?'
Brake Maclean, and his wrath rose red as a beacon the
    wind hath upblown.

· Three does and a ten-tined buck made out,' spoke Hamish,
    full mild,
  'And I ran for to turn, but my breath it was blown, and
    they passed;
  I was weak, for ye called ere I broke me my fast.'
Cried Maclean : 'Now a ten-tined buck in the sight of the
    wife and the child

'I had killed if the gluttonous kern had not wrought me a
    snail's own wrong!'
  Then he sounded, and down came kinsmen and clans-
    men all :
  'Ten blows, for ten tine, on his back let fall,
And reckon no stroke if the blood follow not at the bite of
    thong!'

So Hamish made bare and took him the strokes; at the
    last he smiled.
  'Now I'll to the burn,' quoth Maclean, 'for it still may be

If a slimmer-paunched henchman will hurry with me,
I shall kill me the ten-tined buck for a gift to the wife and
    the child !'

Then the clansmen departed, by this path and that; and
    over the hill
    Sped Maclean with an outward wrath for an inward
      shame;
    And that place of the lashing full quiet became;
And the wife and the child stood sad; and bloody-backed
    Hamish sat still.

But look! red Hamish has risen; quick about and about
    turns he.
    'There is none betwixt me and the crag-top!' he screams
      under breath.
    Then, livid as Lazarus lately from death,
He snatches the child from the mother, and clambers the
    crag toward the sea.

Now the mother drops breath; she is dumb, and her heart
    goes dead for a space,
    Till the motherhood, mistress of death, shrieks, shrieks
      through the glen,
    And that place of the lashing is live with men,
And Maclean, and the gillie that told him, dash up in a
    desperate race.

Not a breath's time for asking; an eye-glance reveals all
    the tale untold.
    They follow mad Hamish afar up the crag toward the sea,

And the lady cries : 'Clansmen, run for a fee ! —
You castle and lands to the two first hands that shall hook
　　him and hold

'Fast Hamish back from the brink !' — and ever she flies
　　up the steep,
　And the clansmen pant, and they sweat, and they jostle
　　　and strain.
　But, mother, 't is vain ; but, father, 't is vain ;
Stern Hamish stands bold on the brink, and dangles the
　　child o'er the deep.

Now a faintness falls on the men that run, and they all
　　stand still.
　And the wife prays Hamish as if he were God, on her
　　　knees,
　Crying : 'Hamish ! O Hamish ! but please, but please
For to spare him !' and Hamish still dangles the child,
　　with a wavering will.

On a sudden he turns ; with a sea-hawk scream, and a gibe,
　　and a song,
　Cries : 'So ; I will spare ye the child if, in sight of ye all,
　Ten blows on Maclean's bare back shall fall,
And ye reckon no stroke if the blood follow not at the bite
　　of the thong !'

Then Maclean he set hardly his tooth to his lip that his
　　tooth was red,
　Breathed short for a space, said : 'Nay, but it shall
　　never be !

Let me hurl off the damnable hound in the sea !'
But the wife : 'Can Hamish go fish us the child from the
    sea, if dead ?

'Say yea ! — Let them lash *me*, Hamish ? ' — ' Nay ! ' —
    ' Husband, the lashing will heal ;
But, oh, who will heal me the bonny sweet bairn in his
    grave ?
Could ye cure me my heart with the death of a knave ?
Quick ! Love ! I will bare thee, so kneel ! '   Then Maclean
    'gan slowly to kneel

With never a word, till presently downward he jerked to
    the earth.
Then the henchman — he that smote Hamish — would
    tremble and lag ;
'Strike, hard ! ' quoth Hamish full stern, from the crag ;
Then he struck him, and ' One ! ' sang Hamish, and danced
    with the child in his mirth.

And no man spake beside Hamish ; he counted each stroke
    with a song.
When the last stroke fell, then he moved him a pace
    down the height,
And he held forth the child in the heartaching sight
Of the mother, and looked all pitiful grave, as repenting a
    wrong.

And there as the motherly arms stretched out with the
    thanksgiving prayer —
And there as the mother crept up with a fearful swift pace,

Till her finger nigh felt of the bairnie's face —
In a flash fierce Hamish turned round and lifted the child
    in the air,

And sprang with the child in his arms from the horrible
    height in the sea,
    Shrill screeching, ' Revenge ! ' in the wind-rush ; and
      pallid Maclean,
    Age-feeble with anger and impotent pain,
Crawled up on the crag, and lay flat, and locked hold of
    dead roots of a tree —

And gazed hungrily o'er, and the blood from his back drip-
    dripped in the brine,
    And a sea-hawk flung down a skeleton fish as he flew,
    And the mother stared white on the waste of the blue,
And the wind drove a cloud to seaward, and the sun began
    to shine.

13

By H. Cholmondeley-Pennell.

THE BOAT–RACE.

THERE 's a living thread that goes winding, winding,
    Tortuous rather, but easy of finding,
        Creep and crawl
        By paling and wall,
    Very much like a dust-dry snake,
    From Hyde Park Corner right out to Mortlake ;
        Crawl and creep
        By level and steep,
From Putney Bridge back again to Eastcheap, —
        Horse and man,
        Wagon and van,
    Tramping along since the day began, —
Rollicking, rumbling, and rolling apace,
With their heads all one way like a shoal of dace ;
        And beauty and grace,
        The lofty and base,
        Silk, satins, and lace,
        And the evil in case,
Seem within an ace of a general embrace —
Jog-trotting behind the Lord Mayor with his mace —
        As if the whole place
        Had set its whole face
Towards the Oxford and Cambridge Race.

Has any one seen some grand, fleet horse,
At the starting-post of an Epsom course,
With nostril spread and chest expanding,
But like a graven image standing,
Waiting a touch to start into life
And spurn the earth in the flying strife;
Whilst around, with restless, eddying pace,
Frolic the froth and foam of the race?
      So, side by side,
      Like shadows they glide,
Two streaks of blue just breasting the tide,
Whilst a thousand oars are glitt'ring wide,
    Flashed in the morning beam, —
And so, when waked to sudden speed,
Darts from the throng the flying steed,
    They darted up the stream.

      With a rush and a bound,
      And a surging sound
From the arches below and the boats around,
And the background of everything wooden and steel
That 's driven by oar, sail, paddle, or wheel,
      Striving and tearing,
      And puffing and swearing,
With the huge live swarm that their decks are bearing, —
A sound from bridge and river and shore,
That gathers into a human roar:
'*Cambridge! Cambridge!*' '*Now, Oxford, now!*'
      Betwixt the crews
      There is n't a pin to choose,
    Not so much as the turn of a 'feather;'

The Cambridge eight
Have muscle and weight,
But the dark blue blades fall sharp and straight
As the hammer of Thor on the anvil of fate,
So wholly they pull together.

And they pull with a will! —
Row, Cambridge, row!
They 're going two lengths to your one, you know, —
The Oxford have got the start —
Out and in, at a single dash —
Flash and feather, feather and flash,
Without a jerk or an effort or splash, —
It 's a stroke that will break your heart —
A wonderful stroke! but a *leetle* too fast?
Forty-four to the minute, at least;
For five or six years it 's been all your own way,
But you 've got your work cut out to-day;
Give them the Cambridge swing, I say,
The grand old stroke, with its sweep and sway,
And send her along! — never mind the spray —
It 's a mercy the pace can't last. . . .
They never can 'stay,' though the Turn is in sight . . .
Ha, now she lifts! — row, row! . . .
But in spite
Of the killing pace, and the stroke of might,
In spite of bone and muscle and height,
On flies the dark blue like a flash of blue light,
And the river froths like yeast. . . .

'Oxford, Oxford! she wins, she wins' —
Well, you 've won 'the toss,' you see,

Whilst the Cantabs must fetch
Their boats thro' a stretch
That 's as lumpy and cross as may be;
And the men are too big, and the boats too small,
For a rushing tide and a racing squall —
But look ! by the bridge, a haven for all —
And Cambridge may win if she can ; —
And the squall 's gone down, and the froth is past.
And you 'll find it 's the 'pace that kills' at last —
You must *pull*, do you understand ?
Put your backs into it — now or never —
Jam home your feet whilst the clenched oars quiver,
For over the gold of the gleaming river
They 're passing you hand over hand :
And a thousand cheers
Ring in their ears —
The muscles stand out on their arms like cords,
Brows knit and teeth close set, —
And bone and weight are beginning to tell,
And the swinging stroke that the Cam knows well
Will lick you yet . . .
Cambridge ! Cambridge again ! Bravo —
Splendidly pulled ; now, Trinity, now, —
Now let the oars sweep, —
Now, whilst the shouts rise,
And the white foam flies,
And the stretched boat seems to leap !
Stick to it, boys, for the bonny light blue . . .
And the turquoise silk, dasht with the spray,
Steals forward now ;
Rowed, rowed of all ! . . .
But what ails the crew ?

What ails the strong arms, unused to wax dull?
And the light boat trails like a wounded gull.

    .   .   .   .

    Swamped! swamped, by heaven!
        Beat in mid-fight,
        With the goal in sight,
    As they were gaining fast;
    Row, Cambridge, row!
    Swamped, while the great crowd roared,
    Wash over wash it poured
        Inch by inch;
        Does a man flinch?
        Row, Cambridge, row!
    Stick to it to the last,
    Over the brown waves' crest
    Only the oarsmen's breast,
        Yet, Cambridge, row;
One gallant stroke, pulled all altogether —
One more! . . . and a long flash in the dark river,
    And the dark blue shoots past.

By Louise Imogen Guiney.

A BALLAD OF METZ.[6]

LÉON went to the wars,
  True soul without a stain;
First at the trumpet-call,
  Thy son, Lorraine!

Never a mighty host
  Thrilled so with one desire;
Never a past Crusade
  Lit nobler fire.

And he, among the rest,
  Smote foeman in the van, —
No braver blood than his
  Since time began.

And mild and fond was he,
  And sensitive as a leaf, —
Just Heaven! that he was this,
  Is half my grief!

We followed where the last
   Detachment led away,
At Metz, an evil-starred
   And bitter day.

Some of us had been hurt
   In the first hot assault,
Yet wills were slackened not,
   Nor feet at fault.

We hurried on to the front;
   Our banners were soiled and rent;
Grim riflemen, gallants all,
   Our captain sent.

A Prussian lay by a tree
   Rigid as ice, and pale,
And sheltered out of the reach
   Of battle-hail.

His cheek was hollow and white,
   Parched was his purple lip;
Tho' bullets had fastened on
   Their leaden grip,

Tho' ever he gasped and called,
   Called faintly from the rear,
What of it?   And all in scorn
   I closed mine ear.

The very colors he wore,
   They burnt and bruised my sight;
The greater his anguish, so
   Was my delight.

We laughed a savage laugh,
  Who loved our land too well,
Giving its enemies hate
  Unspeakable :

But Léon, kind heart, poor heart,
  Clutched me round the arm;
'He faints for water!' he said,
  'It were no harm

'To soothe a wounded man
  Already on death's rack.'
He seized his brimming gourd,
  And hurried back.

The foeman grasped it quick
  With wild eyes, 'neath whose lid
A coiled and viper-like look
  Glittered and hid.

He raised his shattered frame
  Up from the grassy ground,
And drank with the loud, mad haste
  Of a thirsty hound.

Léon knelt by his side,
  One hand beneath his head ;
Not kinder the water than
  The words he said.

He rose and left him so,
  Stretched on the grassy plot,
The viper-like flame in his eyes
  Alas ! forgot.

Léon with easy gait
  Strode on; he bared his hair,
Swinging his army cap,
  Humming an air.

Just as he neared the troops,
  Over there by the stream —
Good God! a sudden snap,
  And a lurid gleam.

I wrenched my bandaged arm
  With the horror of the start :
Léon was low at my feet,
  Shot thro' the heart.

Do you think an angel told
  Whose hand the deed had done ?
To the Prussian we dashed back,
  Mute, every one.

Do you think we stopped to curse,
  Or wailing feebly, stood ?
Do you think we spared who shed
  A friend's sweet blood ?

Ha! vengeance on the fiend :
  We smote him as if hired ;
I most of them, and more
  When they had tired.

I saw the deep eye lose
  Its dastard, steely blue :
I saw the trait'rous breast
  Pierced thro' and thro'.

His musket, smoking yet,
  Unhanded, lay beside;
Three times three thousand deaths
  That Prussian died.

And he, my brother, Léon,
  Lies too upon the plain:
Oh, teach no more Christ's mercy,
  Thy sons, Lorraine!

By Agnes Mary Frances Robinson.

JÜTZI SCHULTHEISS.[6]

Töss, 1300.

THE gift of God was mine; I lost
For aye the gift of Pentecost.

I never knew why God bestowed
On me the vision and the load ;
But what He wills I have no will
To question, blindly following still
The hand that even from my birth
Hath shown me Heaven, forbidding Earth.
I was a child when first I drew
In sight of God ; a subtle, new,
Faint happiness had drawn about
My soul, and shut the whole earth out.
Yet I was sick. I lay in bed,
So weak I could not lift my head, —
So weak, and yet so quite at rest,
Pillowed upon my Saviour's breast
It seemed. Then suddenly I felt
Great wings encompass me, and dwelt
Silent awhile in awe and fear,
While swiftly nearer and more near
Descended God. A stream of white,

Shining, intolerable light
Blinded my eyes, and all grew dim.
Then stilled in trance I dwelt with Him
A little while in perfect peace,
Till, fold by fold, the dark withdrew,
I felt the heavenly blessing cease,
And angels swiftly bear me through
The dizzy air in lightning flight,
Till here I woke and it was night.
My mother wept beside my bed,
My brothers prayed; for I was dead.
Then, when my soul was given back,
I cried, as wretches on the rack
Cry in the last quick wrench of pain,
And breathed, and looked, and lived again.
Ah me, what tears of joy there fell!
How they all cried, 'A miracle!'
And kissed me, given back to earth,
The dearer for that second birth
To her who bore me first. Ah me,
How glad we were! Then Anthony,
My brother, spoke. 'What God has given,'
He said, 'let us restore to Heaven.'
And as he spoke, beneath the rod
I bowed, and gave myself to God.

Not suddenly the gift returned.
Alas! methinks too much I yearned
For the old earthly joys, the home
That I had left forevermore;
The garden with its herbs, and store

Of hives filled full of honeycomb;
The lambs and calves that chiefly were,
Of all we had, my special care;
My brothers, too, all left behind, —
All, for some other girl to find;
And she who loves me everywhere,
My mother, whom I often kissed
In absence with vain lips that missed
My mother more than God above.
Much bound was I with earthly love.
So slight my strength, I never could
Have freed myself from servitude.
But He who loves us saw my pain,
And with one blow struck free my chain.
Weeping I knelt within the gloom,
One evening, in my convent room,
Trying with all my heart to pray,
And weeping that my thoughts would stray;
When suddenly again I felt
The unearthly light and rest; I dwelt
Rapt in mid-heaven the whole night through,
And through my cell the angels flew,
The angels sang, the angels shone.
The Saints in glory, one by one,
Floated to God; and under Him
Circled the shining Seraphim.

Now from that day my heart was free,
And I was God's; then gradually
The convent learned the solemn truth,
And they were glad because my youth

Was pleasing in the sight of Him
Who filled my spirit to the brim.
They wrote my visions down, and made
A treasure of the words I said.
And far and wide the news was spread
That I by God was visited.
Then many sought our convent's door,
And lands and dower began to pour
With blessing on our house; for thus
Men praised the Lord who favored us.

For seven long years the gift was mine:
I often saw the angels shine
Suddenly down the cloister's dark
Deserted length at night; and oft
At the high mass I seemed to mark
A stranger music, high and soft,
That swam about the heavenly Cup,
And caught our ruder voices up;
And often, nay, indeed at will,
I would lie back and let the still
Cold trance creep over me, and see
Mary and all the Saints flash by,
Till only God was left and I.

The gift of God was mine; I lost
For aye the gift of Pentecost.
Now sometimes in the summer-time
I stood beneath the orchard trees,
And in their boughs I heard the breeze
Keep on a low continuing rhyme,

And nothing else was heard beside
The little birds that sang and cried
Their Latin to the praise of God.
And underfoot new grass I trod,
And overhead the light was green,
And all the boughs were starred and gay
With apple-blossoms in between
The fresh young leaves as sweet as they.
And as I looked upon the sun,
Who made these fair things every one
To sprout and sing and wax so strong,
My whole heart turned into a song.
' For, God,' I thought, ' this sun art Thou,
And Thou art in the orchard bough,
And in the grass whereon I tread,
And in the bird-song overhead,
And in my soul and limbs and voice,
And in my heart which must rejoice —
God!' And my song stopped weak and dazed;
I seemed upon the very verge
Of some great brink, wherefrom amazed
My soul shrank back, lest should emerge
Thence — Nay, what then? What should I fear, —
I to whom God was known and dear?

Once so possessed with God, I stood
In prayer within the orchard wood,
When some one softly called my name,
And shattered all my happy mood.
Towards me an ancient Sister came,
' Quick, Jützi, to the hall!' she cried;

And swiftly after her I hied,
And swiftly reached the convent hall,
Now full of struggle and loud with brawl.

Close to the door aghast I stayed,
Too much indignant and afraid
To ask who wrought this blasphemy.
Then the old nun crept nearer me,
And whispered how some knights to-day,
Riding to Zürich's tourney-fray,
Had craved our shelter and repast,
And how we made the postern fast,
Because they were so rough a crew,
Yet gave them food and rest enew
In the great barn outside the gate;
And how they feasted long and late
Till, drunk, they stormed the postern door,
And sacked the buttery for more.
Nor this the end; for having done,
One shouted ' Nassau; ' straightway one
' Hapsburg.' The battle was begun.

She looked at me afraid and faint,
With eyes that mutely begged for aid;
For I was safe and I a saint,
She thought, who was a frightened maid;
And through the clamor and the din
I heard her say, ' They can but sin,
Having not God within their heart;
But we, who have the better part,
Must pray for them to Christ above,

14

That in the greatness of His love
He pardon them their sins to-day.'
And then she turned her eyes away.
But I looked straight before me where
The unseemly blows and clamors were,
And cold my heart grew, stiff and cold,
For I had prayed so much of old,
So vainly for these knights-at-arms,
Who filled the country with alarms —
Too often had I prayed in vain,
Too often put myself in pain
For these irreverent, brawling, rough,
And godless knights — I had prayed enough!

'Let God,' I cried, 'do all He please;
I pray no more for such as these.'
Then swift I turned and fled, as though
I fled from sin, and strife, and woe,
Who fled from God, and from His grace.
Nor stayed I till I reached the place
Where I had prayed an hour ago.

I stood again beneath the shade
The flowering apple-orchard made;
The grass was still as tall and green
And fresh as ever it had been.
I heard the little rabbits rush
As swiftly through the wood; the thrush
Was singing still the self-same song,
Yet something there was changed and wrong.
Or through the grass or through my heart

Some deadly thing had passed athwart,
And left behind a blighting track;
For the old peace comes never back.

God knows how I am humbled, how
There is in all the convent now
No novice half so weak and poor
In all esteem as I: the door
I keep, and wait on passers-by,
And lead the cattle out to browse,
And wash the beggars' feet; even I,
Who was the glory of our house.
Yet dares my soul rejoice, because
Though I have failed, though I have sinned,
Not less eternal are the laws
Of God, no less the sun and wind
Declare His glory than before,
Though I am fallen, and faint, and poor.
Nay, should I fall to very Hell,
Yet am I not so miserable
As heathen are, who know not Him
Who makes all other glories dim.
O God, believed in still though lost,
Yet fill me with Thy Holy Ghost —
Let but the vision fill mine eye
An instant ere the tear be dry;
Or, if Thou wilt, keep hid and far,
Yet art Thou still the secret star
To which my soul sets all her tides, —
My soul, that recks of nought besides.
Have I not found Thee in the fire

Of sunset's purple afterglow?
Have I not found Thee in the throe
Of anguished hearts that bleed and tire, —
God, once so plain to see and hear,
Now never answering any tear?
O God, a guest within my house
Thou wert, my love Thou wert, my spouse:
Yet never known so well as now
When the ash whitens on my brow,
And cinders on my head are tossed,
Because the gift I had I lost.

By Eugene Lee-Hamilton.

SISTER MARY OF THE PLAGUE.

I.

IN her work there is no flagging,
   And her slight frame seems of steel;
And her face and eyes and motions,
Tired by countless nights of watching,
   Nor fatigue nor pain reveal.

Yet the Sisters say she eats not,
   Spurning food as ne'er did saint;
And they murmur, ' She is nourished
By a miracle of Heaven;
   God allows not she should faint.'

Through the darkened wards she passes
   On her round from bed to bed;
And the sick who wait her coming
Cease their groaning, smiling faintly
   As they hear her light quick tread.

Through the gabled lanes she hurries;
   And the ribald men-at-arms
Hush their mirth, and, stepping backward,
Let her pass to soothe some death-bed,
   Safe from insults and alarms;

And the priests and monks and townsfolk
  Whom she passes greet her sight
With a strange respectful pleasure,
As she nears in dark blue flannel
  And huge cap of spotless white.

Oh, the busy Flemish City
  Knows its Sister Mary well;
And the very children show her
To the stranger as she passes,
  And her story all can tell:

How she won a lasting glory,
  Cleaving to the dread bedside
When the Plague with livid pinions
Lighted on the crowded alleys,
  And all others fled or died.

How alone she made men listen
  In their fear, and do her will;
Making help and making order
When the customary rulers
  Trembled hopeless, and stood still.

How she had the corpses buried
  When they choked canal and street;
When alone the shackled convicts,
Goaded on with pike and halberd,
  Cared to near with quaking feet.

Sister Mary of the Plague.

But those days of fear are over;
    And the pure canal reflects
Barges decked with pots of flowers
And long rows of tile-faced gables,
    Which no breeze of death infects.

And once more the city prospers
    Through the cunning of its guilds;
While the restless shuttles clatter,
And in peace the busy Fleming
    Weaves and tans and brews and builds;

And the bearded Spanish troopers,
    Sitting idly in the shade,
Toss their dice with oath and rattle,
Or crack jokes with girls that pass them,
    Laughing-eyed and unafraid.

II.

Sister Mary, Sister Mary,
    In thy soul there is some change :
For thy face the while thou watchest
By a pale young Spanish soldier
    Works with struggle strong and strange.

Thou hast watched a hundred death-beds,
    Ever calm, without dismay;
Fighting like a steady fighter
While the shade of Death pressed onward
    Night on night and day on day;

And when Death had proved the stronger,
　Thou wouldst heave one sigh at most,
And then turn to some new moaner,
Ready to resume the battle,
　Just as steady at thy post.

Now thy soul is filled with anguish
　Strange and wild, thou know'st not why;
While a voice unknown and inward
Seems to whisper, far and faintly,
　' If he dies, thou too wilt die.'

Many months has he been lying
　In thy ward, and rises not;
Youth and strength avail him nothing;
Growing daily whiter, whiter;
　Dying of men know not what.

And he murmurs : ' Sister Mary,
　Now the end is nearing fast;
Thou hast nursed me like God's Angel
But the hand of God is on me,
　And thy care must end at last.

' I have few, few days remaining;
　Now I scarce can draw my breath;
See my hand : no blood is in it ;
And I feel like one who slowly,
　Slowly, slowly bleeds to death.'

And his worn and heavy eyelids
  Close again as if in sleep;
While thou lookest at his features
With a long and searching anguish
  In thy eyes — that dare not weep.

Sister Mary, Sister Mary,
  Watch him closer, closer still!
There be things within the boundless
Realm of Horror, unsuspected, —
  Things that slowly, slowly kill!

In his face there is no color,
  And his hand is ivory-white;
But upon his throat is something
Like a small red stain or puncture,
  Something like a leech's bite.

Sister Mary, Sister Mary,
  Dost thou see that small red stain?
Hast thou never noticed something
Like it on the throats of others
  Whom thy care has nursed in vain?

Have no rumors reached thee, Sister,
  Of a Thing that haunts these wards
When the scanty sleep thou takest
Cheats the sick of the protection
  Which thy vigilance affords?

When, at night, the ward is silent,
  And the night-lamp's dimness hides,
And the nurse on duty slumbers
In her chair with measured breathing,
  Then it glides, and glides, and glides,

Like a woman's form, new risen
  From the grave with soundless feet,
Clad in something which the shadows
Of the night-lamp render doubtful
  Whether robe or winding-sheet.

And its eyes seem fixed and sightless,
  Like the eyeballs of the dead ;
But it gropes not, and moves onward
Sure and silent, seeking something
  In the ward, from bed to bed.

And if any, lying sleepless,
  Sees it, he becomes as stone ;
Terror glues his lips together,
While his eyes are forced to follow
  All its movements, one by one.

And he sees it stop, and hover
  Round a bed, with wavering will,
Like a bat which, ere it settles,
Flits in circles ever smaller,
  Nearer, nearer, nearer still.

Then it bends across the sleeper
    Restless in the sultry night,
And begins to fan him gently
With its garment, till his slumber
    Groweth deep, and dreamless quite;

And its corpse-like face unstiffens
    And its dead eyes seem to gloat
As, approaching and approaching,
It applies its mouth of horror
    Slowly, firmly, to his throat.

Sister Mary, Sister Mary,
    Has no rumor told thee this?
What if he whose life thou lovest
Like thine own, and more, were dying
    Of that long terrific kiss?

III.

From the Hospital's arched window,
    Open to the summer air,
You can see the monks in couples
All returning home at sunset
    Through the old cathedral square.

On the steps of the cathedral,
    In the weak declining sun
Sit the beggars and the cripples;
While faint gusts of organ-rolling
    Tell that vespers have begun.

Slowly creeps the tide of shadow
   Up the steps of sculptured front,
Driving back the yellow sunshine
On each pinnacle and buttress
   Which the twilight soon makes blunt.

Slowly evening grasps the city,
   And the square grows still and lone;
No one passes save, it may be,
Up the steps and through the portal,
   Some stray monk or tottering crone.

In this room, which seems the study
   Of the Hospital's chief leech,
There is no one; but the twilight
Makes all objects seem mysterious,
   Like a conscious watcher each.

Here the snakes whose venom healeth
   Stand in jars in hideous file;
While the skulls that crown the book-shelves
Seem to grin; and from the ceiling
   Hangs the huge stuffed crocodile.

Here be kept the drugs and cordials
   Which the Jew from Syria brings,
And perchance drugs yet more precious,
Melted topaz, pounded ruby,
   Such as save the lives of kings.

All is silent in the study;
  But the door-hinge creaks anon,
And a woman enters softly
Seeking something that seems hidden, —
  One unnaturally wan.

What she seeks is not in phials
  Nor in jars, but in a book;
And she mutters as she searches
Through the book-shelves with a kind of
  Brooding hurry in her look;

And she finds the book, and takes it
  To the window for more light;
And she reads a passage slowly,
With constrained and hissing breathing,
  And dark brow contracted tight.

' *Most of them,*' it says, ' *are corpses*
  That have lain beneath the moon,
And that quit their graves at midnight,
Prowling round to prey on sleepers;
  But the daybreak scares them soon.

' *But the worst, called soulless bodies,*
  Plague the world but now and then;
They have died in some great sickness;
But reviving in the moonbeams
  Rise once more and mix with men.

' *And they act and feel like others,*
　　Never guessing they be dead,
Common food of men they love not;
But at night, impelled by hunger,
　　In their sleep they quit their bed;

And they fasten on some sleeper,
　　Feeding on his living blood;
Who, when life has left his body,
Must in turn arise, and, prowling,
　　Seek the like accursed food.'

And the book slips from her fingers,
　　And she casts her down to pray;
But convulsions seize and twist her,
And delirious ramblings mingle
　　With the prayers she tries to say.

In her mouth there is a saltness,
　　On her lips there is a stain;
In her soul there is a horror;
In her vitals there is something
　　More like raging thirst than pain;

And she cries, 'O God, I knew it:
　　Have I not at dead of night,
Waking up, looked round and found me
On the ledge of roofs and windows
　　In my shift, and shrunk with fright?

'Have I not, O God of mercy,
  Passed by shambles in the street,
And stopped short in monstrous craving
For the crimson blood that trickled
  In the gutter at my feet?

'Did I not, at last Communion,
  Cough the Holy Wafer out?
Blood I suck, but Christ's blood chokes me.
O my God, my God, vouchsafe me
  Some strong light in this great doubt!'

And she sinketh crushed and prostrate
  In the twilight on the floor,
While the darkness grows around her,
And her quick and labored breathing
  Grows convulsive more and more.

IV.

Sister Mary, all is quiet
  In thy wards, and midnight nears:
Seek the scanty rest thou needest;
Seek the scanty rest thou grudgest;
  All is hushed and no one fears.

But, though midnight, Sister Mary
  Thinks it yet not time to go;
And the night-lamps shining dimly
Show her vaguely in the shadow
  Moving softly to and fro.

What is it that she is doing,
    Flitting round one sleeper's bed, —
Is she sprinkling something round it,
Something white as wheaten flour,
    And on which she will not tread ?

And at last the work is over,
    And she goeth to her rest ;
And she sleeps at once, exhausted
By ·long labor, and, it may be,
    By strong struggles in her breast.

Nothing breaks upon the stillness
    Of the night, except, afar,
Some faint shouts of ending revel,
Or of brawling, in the quarters
    Where the Spanish soldiers are.

Time wades slowly through the darkness
    Till at last it reaches day,
And the city's many steeples,
Buried in the starless heaven,
    Grow distinct in sunless grey.

And the light wakes Sister Mary,
    And she dresses in strange haste,
Giving God no prayer, and leaving
On her bed the beads and crosses
    That should dangle from her waist.

And with unheard steps she hurries
  Through the ward where all sleep on,
To the bed in which is lying
He who day by day is growing
  More inexorably wan.

All around the bed is sprinkled
  Something white, like thin fresh snow,
Where a naked foot has printed
In the night a many footprints,
  Sharp and clear from heel to toe.

Sister Mary, Sister Mary,
  Dost thou know thy own small foot?
Would it fit these marks which make thee
Turn more pale than thy own paleness
  If upon them it were put?

And the dying youth smiles faintly
  Pleasure's last accorded smile;
And he murmurs, as he hears her,
'Sister Mary, I am better;
  Let me hold thy hand awhile;

'Sister Mary, I would tell thee
  Fain one thing before I die;
For a dying man may utter
What another must keep hidden
  In the fastness of a sigh.

'Sister Mary, I have loved thee —
   Is it sin to tell thee this ?
And I dreamt — O God, be lenient
   If 't is sin — that thou didst give me
      On the throat a long, long kiss.'

By May Kendall.

BALLAD.

HE said: ' The shadows darken down,
   The night is near at hand.
Now who 's the friend will follow me
   Into the sunless land ?

' For I have vassals leal and true,
   And I have comrades kind,
And wheresoe'er my soul shall speed,
   They will not stay behind.'

He sought the brother young and blithe
   Who bore his spear and shield :
' In the long chase you 've followed me,
   And in the battle-field.

' Few vows you make; but true 's your heart,
   And you with me will win.'
He said: ' God speed you, brother mine,
   But I am next of kin.'

He sought the friar, the grey old priest
   Who loved his father's board.
The friar he turned him to the east
   And reverently adored.

He said : 'A godless name you bear,
　A godless life you 've led,
And whoso wins along with you,
　His spirit shall have dread.

'Oh, hasten, get your guilty soul
　From every burden shriven ;
Yet you are bound for flame and dole,
　But I am bound for heaven !'

He sought the lady bright and proud,
　Who sate at his right hand :
' Make haste, O Love, to follow me
　Into the sunless land.'

She said : 'And pass you in your prime ?
　Heaven give me days of cheer!
And keep me from the sunless clime
　Many and many a year.'

All heavily the sun sank down
　Among black clouds of fate.
There came a woman fair and wan
　Unto the castle gate.

Through gazing vassals, idle serfs,
　So silently she sped !
The winding staircase echoed not
　Unto her light, light tread.

His lady eyed her scornfully.
　She stood at his right hand ;
She said : 'And I will follow you
　Into the sunless land.

'There is no expiation, none.
  A bitter load I bore :
Now I shall love you nevermore,
  Never and nevermore.

'There is no touch or tone of yours
  Can make the old love wake.'
She said : ' But I will follow you,
  Even for the old love's sake.'

Oh, he has kissed her on the brow,
  He took her by the hand :
Into the sunless land they went,
  Into the starless land.

By George Meredith.

THE YOUNG PRINCESS.

A BALLAD OF OLD LAWS OF LOVE.

I.

WHEN the South sang like a nightingale
  Above a bower in May,
The training of Love's vine of flame
Was writ in laws, for lord and dame
  To say their yea and nay.

When the South sang like a nightingale
  Across the flowering night,
And lord and dame held gentle sport,
There came a young princess to Court,
  A frost of beauty white.

The South sang like a nightingale
  To thaw her glittering dream:
No vine of Love her bosom gave,
She drank no vine of Love, but grave
  She held them to Love's theme.

The South grew all a nightingale
  Beneath a moon unmoved:
Like the banner of war she led them on;
She left them to die, like the light that has gone
  From wine-cups over proved.

When the South was a fervid nightingale,
  And she a chilling moon,
'T was a pity to see on the garden swards,
Against Love's laws, those rival lords
  As willow-wands lie strewn.

The South had throat of a nightingale
  For her, the young princess :
She gave no vine of Love to rear,
Love's wine drank not, yet bent her ear
  To themes of Love no less.

II.

The lords of the Court they sighed heart-sick ;
  Heart-free Lord Dusiote laughed :
' I prize her no more than a fling o' the dice,
But, or shame to my manhood, a lady of ice,
  We master her by craft ! '

Heart-sick the lords of joyance yawned ;
  Lord Dusiote laughed heart-free :
' I count her as much as a crack o' my thumb,
But, or shame of my manhood, to me she shall come
  Like the bird to roost in the tree ! '

At dead of night, when the palace-guard
  Had passed the measured rounds,
The young princess awoke to feel
A shudder of blood at the crackle of steel
  Within the garden-bounds.

It ceased, and she thought of whom was need,
  The friar or the leech;
When lo! stood her tire-woman breathless by:
' Lord Dusiote, Madam, to death is nigh,
  Of you he would have speech.

' He prays you of your gentleness
  To light him to his dark end.'
The princess rose, and forth she went,
For charity was her intent,
  Devoutly to befriend.

Lord Dusiote hung on his good squire's arm,
  The priest beside him knelt:
A weeping handkerchief was pressed,
To stay the red flood at his breast,
  And bid cold ladies melt.

' O lady, though you are ice to men,
  All pure to heaven as light
Within the dew within the flower,
Of you 't is whispered that love has power
  When secret is the night.

' I have silenced the slanderers, peace to their souls!
  Save one was too cunning for me.
I die, whose love is late avowed,
He lives, who boasts the lily has bowed
  To the oath of a bended knee.'

Lord Dusiote drew breath with pain,
  And she with pain drew breath :
On him she looked, on his like above;
She flew in the folds of a marvel of love,
  Revealed to pass to death.

' You are dying, O great-hearted lord,
  You are dying for me,' she cried;
' Oh, take my hand, oh, take my kiss,
And take of your right for love like this
  The vow that plights me bride.'

She bade the priest recite his words
  While hand in hand were they,
Lord Dusiote's soul to waft to bliss ;
He had her hand, her vow, her kiss,
  And his body was borne away.

III.

Lord Dusiote sprang from priest and squire ;
  He gazed at her lighted room :
The laughter in his heart grew slack ;
He knew not the force that pushed him back
  From her and the morn in bloom.

Like a drowned man's length on the strong flood-tide,
  Like the shade of a bird in the sun,
He fled from his lady whom he might claim
As ghost, and who made the daybeams flame
  To scare what he had done.

There was grief at Court for one so gay,
　Though he was a lord less keen
For training the vine than at vintage-press ;
But in her soul the young princess
　Believed that love had been.

Lord Dusiote fled the Court and land,
　He crossed the woful seas,
Till his traitorous doing seemed clearer to burn,
And the lady beloved drew his heart for return,
　Like the banner of war in the breeze.

He neared the palace, he spied the Court,
　And music he heard, and they told
Of foreign lords arrived to bring
The nuptial gifts of a bridegroom king
　To the princess grave and cold.

The masque and dance were cloud on wave,
　And down the masque and the dance
Lord Dusiote stepped from dame to dame,
And to the young princess he came,
　With a bow and a burning glance.

' Do you take a new husband to-morrow, lady ? '
　She shrank as at prick of steel.
' Must the first yield place to the second ? ' he sighed.
Her eyes were like the grave that is wide
　For the corpse from head to heel.

' My lady, my love, that little hand
　　Has mine ringed fast in plight:
I bear for your lips a lawful thirst,
And as justly the second should follow the first,
　　I come to your door this night.'

· If a ghost should come a ghost will go : '
　　No more the lady said,
Save that ever when he in wrath began
To swear by the faith of a living man,
　　She answered him, ' You are dead.'

IV.

The soft night-wind went laden to death
　　With smell of the orange in flower;
The light leaves prattled to neighbor ears;
The bird of the passion sang over his tears;
　　The night waned hour by hour.

Sang loud, sang low the rapturous bird
　　Till the yellow hour was nigh,
Behind the folds of a darker cloud :
He chuckled, he sobbed, alow, aloud, —
　　The voice between earth and sky.

' Oh, will you, nill you, women are weak ;
　　The proudest are yielding mates
For a forward foot and a tongue of fire : '
So thought Lord Dusiote's trusty squire,
　　At watch by the palace-gates.

The song of the bird was wine in his blood,
  And woman the odorous bloom ;
His master's great adventure stirred
Within him to mingle the bloom and bird,
  And morn ere its coming illume.

Beside him strangely a piece of the dark
  Had moved, and the undertones
Of a priest in prayer, like a cavernous wave.
He heard, as were there a soul to save
  For urgency now in the groans.

No priest was hired for the play this night :
  And the squire tossed head like a deer
At sniff of the tainted wind ; he gazed
Where cresset-lamps in a door were raised
  Belike on a passing bier.

All cloaked and masked, with naked blades,
  That flashed of a judgment done,
The lords of the Court, from the palace-door,
Came issuing silently, bearers four,
  And flat on their shoulders one.

They marched the body to squire and priest,
  They lowered it sad to earth :
The priest they gave the burial dole,
Bade wrestle hourly for his soul,
  Who was a lord of worth.

The Young Princess.

One said, ' Farewell to a gallant knight ! '
  And one, ' But a restless ghost !
'T is a year and a day since in this place
He died, sped high by a lady of grace
  To join the blissful host.

' Not vainly on us she charged her cause,
  The lady whom we revere
For faith in the mask of a love untrue
To the Love we honor, the Love her due,
  The Love we have vowed to rear.

' A trap for the sweet tooth, lures for the light,
  For the fortress defiant a mine :
Right well ! But not in the South, princess,
Shall the lady snared of her nobleness
  Ever shamed or a captive pine.'

When the South had voice of a nightingale
  Above a Maying bower,
On the heights of Love walked radiant peers ;
The bird of the passion sang over his tears
  To the breeze and the orange-flower.

By Sir Edwin Arnold.

'A RAJPŬT NURSE.'

' WHOSE tomb have they builded, Vittoo, under this tama-
        rind-tree,
With its door of the rose-veined marble, and white dome
        stately to see, —
Was he holy Brahman, or Yogi, or Chief of the Rajpût line,
Whose urn rests here by the river, in the shade of the
        beautiful shrine?'

' May it please you,' quoth Vittoo, salaaming, ' Protector of
        all the poor!
It was not for holy Brahman they carved that delicate door;
Nor for Yogi, nor Rajpût Rana, built they this gem of our
        land;
But to tell of a Rajpût woman, as long as the stones should
        stand.

'Her name was Môti, the pearl-name; 'twas far in the
        ancient times;
But her moon-like face and her teeth of pearls are sung of
        still in our rhymes;
And because she was young, and comely, and of good
        repute, and had laid
A babe in the arms of her husband,[1] the Palace-Nurse she
        was made.

---

[1] A Hindu father acknowledges paternity by receiving in his arms a
new-born child.

' For the sweet chief queen of the Rana in Jondhpore city
    had died,
Leaving a motherless infant, the heir to that race of pride :
The heir of the peacock-banner, of the five-colored flag,
    of the throne
Which traces its record of glory from days when it ruled
    alone ;

' From times when, forth from the sunlight,[1] the first of
    our kings came down
And had the earth for his footstool, and wore the stars for
    his crown,
As all good Rajpûts have told us ; so Môti was proud and
    true,
With the Prince of the land on her bosom, and her own
    brown baby too.

' And the Rajpût women will have it (I know not myself of
    these things)
As the two babes lay in her lap there, her lord's, and the
    Jondhpore King's,
So loyal was the blood of her body, so fast the faith of her
    heart,
It passed to her new-born infant, who took of her trust its
    part.

' He would not suck of the breast-milk till the Prince had
    drunken his fill;
He would not sleep to the cradle-song till the Prince was
    lulled and still ;

---

1 The Rajpût dynasty is said to be descended from the sun.

And he lay at night with his small arms clasped round the
    Rana's child,
As if those hands like the rose-leaf could shelter from trea-
    son wild.

' For treason was wild in the country, and villanous men
    had sought
The life of the heir of the gadi,[1] to the Palace in secret
    brought ;
With bribes to the base, and with knife-thrusts for the
    faithful, they made their way
Through the line of the guards, and the gateways, to the
    hall where the women lay.

' There Môti, the foster-mother, sat singing the children
    to rest,
Her baby at play on her crossed knees, and the King's
    son held to her breast ;
And the dark slave-maidens round her beat low on the
    cymbal's skin,
Keeping the time of her soft song — when — Saheb! —
    there hurried in

' A breathless watcher, who whispered, with horror in eyes
    and face :
"Oh, Môti! men come to murder my Lord the Prince
    in this place !
They have bought the help of the gate-guards, or slaugh-
    tered them unawares ;
Hark! that is the noise of their tulwars,[2] the clatter upon
    the stairs ! "

[1] The 'seat,' or throne.   [2] Indian swords.

'For one breath she caught her baby from her lap to her
    heart, and let
The King's child sink from her nipple, with lips still cling-
    ing and wet,
Then tore from the Prince his head-cloth, and the putta of
    pearls from his waist,
And bound the belt on her infant, and the cap on his brows,
    in haste ;

'And laid her own dear offspring, her flesh and blood, on
    the floor,
With the girdle of pearls around him, and the cap that the
    King's son wore ;
While close to her heart, which was breaking, she folded
    the Râja's joy,
And — even as the murderers lifted the purdah — she fled
    with his boy.

'But there (so they deemed) in his jewels, lay the Chota
    Rana,[1] the heir ;
"The cow with two calves has escaped us," cried one, "it
    is right and fair
She should save her own butcha ;[2] no matter ! the edge of
    the dagger ends
This spark of Lord Raghoba's sunlight ; stab thrice and
    four times, O friends ! "

'And the Rajpût women will have it (I know not if this
    can be so)
That Môti's son in the putta and golden cap cooed low

---

[1] 'Little King.'   [2] 'Little one.'

When the sharp blades met in his small heart, with never
    one moan or wince,   .
But died with a babe's light laughter, because he died for
    his Prince.

'Thereby did that Rajpût mother preserve the line of our
    Kings.'
'Oh, Vittoo,' I said, 'but they gave her much gold and
    beautiful things,
And garments and land for her people, and a home in the
    Palace!   May be
She had grown to love that Princeling even more than the
    child on her knee.'

'May it please the Presence,' quoth Vittoo, 'it seemeth
    not so! they gave
The gold and the garments and jewels, as much as the
    proudest would have;
But the same night deep in her true heart she buried a
    knife, and smiled,
Saying this: "I have saved my Rana! I must go to suckle
    my child!"'

By Margaret J. Preston.

LADY YEARDLEY'S GUEST.[7]

1654.

'T WAS a Saturday night, midwinter,
  And the snow with its sheeted pall
Had covered the stubbled clearings
  That girdled the rude-built ' Hall.'
But high in the deep-mouthed chimney,
  'Mid laughter and shout and din,
The children were piling yule-logs
  To welcome the Christmas in.

' Ah, so! We 'll be glad to-morrow,'
  The mother half-musing said,
As she looked at the eager workers,
  And laid on a sunny head
A touch as of benediction, —
  ' For Heaven is just as near
The father at far Patuxent
  As if he were with us here.

' So choose ye the pine and holly,
  And shake from their boughs the snow;
We 'll garland the rough-hewn rafters
  As they garlanded long ago, —

Or ever Sir George went sailing
    Away o'er the wild sea-foam, —
In my beautiful English Sussex,
    The happy old walls at home.'

She sighed. As she paused, a whisper
    Set quickly all eyes astrain :
' *See ! See !* ' — and the boy's hand pointed —
    ' *There 's a face at the window-pane !* '
One instant a ghastly terror
    Shot sudden her features o'er ;
The next, and she rose unblenching,
    And opened the fast-barred door.

Who be ye that seek admission ?
    Who cometh for food and rest ?
This night is a night above others
    To shelter a straying guest.'
Deep out of the snowy silence
    A guttural answer broke :
' I came from the great Three Rivers,
    I am Chief of the Roanoke.'

Straight in through the frightened children,
    Unshrinking, the red man strode,
And loosed on the blazing hearthstone,
    From his shoulder, a light-borne load ;
And out of the pile of deer-skins,
    With look as serene and mild
As if it had been in its cradle,
    Stepped softly a four-year child.

As he chafed at the fire his fingers,
  Close pressed to the brawny knee,
The gaze that the silent savage
  Bent on him was strange to see ;
And then, with a voice whose yearning
  The father could scarcely stem,
He said, to the children pointing,
  ' I want him to be like *them* !

' They weep for the boy in the wigwam :
  I bring him, a moon of days,
To learn of the speaking paper ;
  To hear of the wiser ways
Of the people beyond the water ;
  To break with the plough the sod :
To be kind to pappoose and woman ;
  To pray to the white man's God.'

' I give thee my hand ! '   And the lady
  Pressed forward with sudden cheer :
' Thou shalt eat of my English pudding,
  And drink of my Christmas beer.
My darlings, this night, remember
  All strangers are kith and kin, —
This night when the dear Lord's Mother
  Could find no room at the inn.

        .   .   .   .

Next morn from the colony belfry
  Pealed gayly the Sunday chime,
And merrily forth the people
  Flocked, keeping the Christmas time :

And the lady, with bright-eyed children
  Behind her, their lips a-smile,
And the chief in his skins and wampum,
  Came walking the narrow aisle.

Forthwith from the congregation
  Broke fiercely a sullen cry :
'*Out! out! with the crafty red-skin!*
  Have at him! A spy! A spy!'
And quickly from belts leaped daggers,
  And swords from their sheaths flashed bare,
And men from their seats defiant
  Sprang, ready to slay him there.

But facing the crowd with courage
  As calm as a knight of yore,
Stepped bravely the fair-browed woman
  The thrust of the steel before ;
And spake with a queenly gesture,
  Her hand on the chief's brown breast :
'*Ye dare not impeach my honor!*
  Ye dare not insult my guest!'

They dropped, at her word, their weapons,
  Half-shamed as the lady smiled,
And told them the red man's story,
  And showed them the red man's child ;
And pledged them her broad plantations,
  That never would such betray
The trust that a Christian woman
  Had shown on a Christmas Day!

By Stopford A. Brooke.

THE KING AND THE HUNTSMAN.

THE king and his huntsman are gone to the chase,
    And the huntsman's son with them;
Two nights they lay, and two days they rode,
    Till they came to the forest's hem.

'Oh, what are these meadows,' the king he said,
    'And this stream that runs in flood;
And why is the grass as green as a corpse,
    And the stream as red as blood?

'Is this the meadow and this the stream,'
    And he laughed both loud and free:
Where it's twenty years I loved a maid,
    And sorely she loved me?'

Then up and spake the huntsman dark,
    And he was deadly fell.
'Now draw your dagger, my son,' he said,
    'And send this king to hell.

'Revenge burns slow, but it flames at last —
    The maiden was my daughter,
She broke her heart for thee and shame,
    And died in this wild water.

'Nor wife nor child, but the carrion crow
    Shall hear thy dying groan,
And Ellen's stream shall be red with thy blood,
    And the wolves strip thy breastbone.'

Then the king grew pale as the snow at dawn,
    And he bared his hunting-knife;
'Oh, woe that I left my good deer-hound,
    For I should not lose my life.'

'I slew him first,' the huntsman said,
    And fierce at the king he ran;
Strike down at his back, my son, strike hard,
    For he shall not die like a man.'

And they washed their hands in the red, red blood,
    And over the seas to Spain;
And the only sextons that buried the king
    Were the wild beasts and the rain.

By A. C. Gordon.

BEFORE THE PARTY.

YES, honey, you p'int'ly is purty ;
   How long 'fo' de ball gwi' begin ?
'Some time yet ? ' An' when you 's all dancin',
   Can't yer ole Mammy come an' peep in ?

Dat white silk, it sho'ly do suit you —
   An' dem vi'lets wropt inter yer hyar ;
Mars' Ranny loves dem sort o' blossoms —
   I 'spec', Baby, dat 's why dey 's dar.

Lord, chile ! you looks jes' like yer mother.
   When you turn yer head sideways, dat way ;
Has you been showed yerself ter ole Marster ?
   You has, hey ? An' what did he say ?

' He never said nothin' — jes' only
   His mouf twich like ketchin' a cry ;
An' he kissed you, an' turn off an' lef' you,
   Wid de water done come ter his eye ? '

Yes, honey, you 's like her : dat 's gospel ;
   An' I knows, by de way dat he done,
Dat you fotch her up ter him adzactly,
   An' de ole times dat 's over an' gone.

She used ter w'ar vi'lets dat summer —
  He loved 'em, like Mars' Ranny do —
Her fus' season at de White Suff'rer,
  When she was a young gal like you.

I went wid her dar, dat ar season —
  Dey called her de Belle o' de Springs;
De young bucks run crazy about her —
  You never did see sich fool things!

But Marster was dar, de bes'-lookin'
  An' de smartes', I hearn 'em all say;
An' he owned a Jeems River plantation,
  An' so he jes' kerried de day.

She w'ared a white dress de fus' ebenin'
  She danced at de ball; an' she hel'
Some vi'lets like dem in her fingers —
  I 'members it all very well.

I has n't no doubt dat ole Marster,
  When he seed you, he thought o' dat night;
An' mebbe some other times, honey,
  When he 'membered her 'rayed out in white.

Now I thinks, she was drest de same fashion
  At de weddin' at Springfield, you know;
Some vi'lets de onlies' color,
  An' her white silk mo' shiny dan snow;

An', Baby, her fingers wropt over
  Fresh blossoms, fotch f'om de ole place,
Like dem ; an' white garmen's was on her,
  De las' time I looked at her face.

It do make me feel sorter ole-like,
  Fur ter see you growed hansum an' tall ;
I hardly considered it, honey,
  'Twel you fixed up ter 'ten' yer fus' ball —

'Ca'se you 's never seemed nothin' but Baby,
  An' it looks sich a short time ago :
Yes, Mistis, I 'm gwi' come an' see you,
  When you dances wid Mars' Ranny, sho'.

NOTES AND INDEXES.

AUTHORS' NOTES.

NOTE 1, page 31. *The Doncaster St. Leger.* 'This poem is intended to illustrate the spirit of Yorkshire racing, now un-
happily, or happily, as the case may be, on the decline. The
perfect acquaintance of every peasant on the ground with the
pedigrees, performances, and characters of the horses en-
gaged, his genuine interest in the result, and the mixture of
hatred and contempt which he used to feel for the Newmarket favorites who came down to carry off his great natural
prize, must be well known to any one who forty years ago
crossed the Trent in August or September. Altogether it
constituted a peculiar modification of English feeling, which
I thought deserved to be recorded; and in default of a more
accomplished Pindar, I have here endeavored to do so.' To
line 17, page 32, 'When, strong of heart, the Wentworth Bay,'
the author has the following explanatory note: 'Bay Malton,
King Herod, the champion of Newmarket in the famous race
alluded to above, broke a blood-vessel in the crisis of the
contest.'

NOTE 2, page 39. *Winstanley.* 'This ballad was intended to
be one of a set, and was read to the children in the National
Schools at Sherborne, Dorsetshire, in order to discover
whether, if the actions of a hero were simply and plainly
narrated, English children would like to learn by heart the
verses recording them, as their forefathers did.'

NOTE 3, page 117. *The Pearl of the Philippines.* 'This apologue, or the germ of it, will be found in the narrative of a French writer, who claimed to have resided for upward of twenty years in the Philippines, and to have derived it from a native. The *motif* is different in the original, where the vow was made in order to obtain the love of a woman, and not to save the life of a child.'

NOTE 4, page 146. *The King's Tragedy.* 'Tradition says that Catherine Douglas, in honor of her heroic act when she barred the door with her arm against the murderers of James the First of Scots, received popularly the name of "Barlass." The name remains to her descendants, the Barlas family, in Scotland, who bear for their crest a broken arm. She married Alexander Lovell of Bolunnie. A few stanzas from King James's lovely poem known as *The King's Quhair*, are quoted in the course of the ballad. The writer must express regret for the necessity which has compelled him to shorten the ten-syllabled lines to eight syllables, in order that they might harmonize with the ballad metre.'

NOTE 5, page 199. *Ballad of Metz.* 'This incident actually befell a private in a Massachusetts Volunteer regiment, belonging to the Fifth Corps, at the battle of Malvern Hill.'

NOTE 6, page 204. *Jützi Schultheiss.* 'Jützi Schultheiss, a Mediæval Mystic, loses her gift of trance and vision, because in a moment of anger she refuses to pray for some turbulent knights.'

NOTE 7, page 243. *Lady Yeardley's Guest.* 'Sir George Yeardley was Governor of the Colony of Virgina in 1626.'

BIBLIOGRAPHICAL NOTES.

Azenor, by Lewis Morris, page 180. *Songs Unsung*, 1883.

Ballad, by May Kendall, page 227. *Dreams to Sell*, 1887.

Ballad of Isobel, by John Payne, page 126. *New Poems*, 1880.

Ballad of Judas Iscariot (The), by Robert Buchanan, page 88. *Poetical Works*, 1874.

Ballad of Metz (A), by Louise Imogen Guiney, page 199. *Songs at the Start*, 1884.

Ballad of the Thulian Nurse, by George Macdonald, page 27. *Alec Forbes of Howglen*, 1865.

Before Sedan, by Henry Austin Dobson, page 86. *Vignettes in Rhyme and Vers de Société*, 1873.

Before the Party, by A. C. Gordon, page 249. *Befor' de War: Echoes in Negro Dialect*, 1888.

Boat-Race (The), by H. Cholmondeley-Pennell, page 194. '*From Grave to Gay,*' 1884.

Courtin' (The), by James Russell Lowell, page 17. *The Biglow Papers, Second Series*, 1864.

Death of th' Owd Squire (The), by George Walter Thornbury, page 80. *Historical and Legendary Ballads and Songs*, 1873.

Dickens in Camp, by Francis Bret Harte, page 78. *Poems*, 1871.

Doncaster St. Leger (The), by Sir Francis Hastings Charles Doyle, page 31. *The Return of the Guards, and other Poems*, 1866.

Doorstep (The), by Edmund Clarence Stedman, page 57. *The Blameless Prince, and other Poems*, 1869.

First Quarrel (The), by Lord Tennyson, page 140. *Ballads and other Poems*, 1880.

Forced Recruit (The), by Elizabeth Barrett Browning, page 13. *Last Poems*, 1862.

Gulf (The), by Emily Davis Pfeiffer, page 110. *Poems*, 1876.

Hajarlis, by Richard Hengist Horne, page 101. *Cosmo de Medici, An Historical Tragedy, and other Poems*, 1875.

Haystack in the Floods (The), by William Morris, page 1. *The Defence of Guenevere, and other Poems*, 1858.

Hervé Riel, by Robert Browning, page 104. *Pacchiarotto, and how he worked in Distemper: with other Poems*, 1876.

In School-Days, by John Greenleaf Whittier, page 66. *Miriam and other Poems*, 1871.

Jessie Cameron, by Christina Georgina Rossetti, page 59. *The Prince's Progress, and other Poems*, 1870.

Jützi Schultheiss, by Agnes Mary Frances Robinson, page 204. *The New Arcadia, and other Poems*, 1884.

King and the Huntsman (The), by Stopford A. Brooke, page 247. *Poems*, 1888.

King's Tragedy (The), by Gabriel Charles Dante Rossetti, page 146. *Ballads and Sonnets*, 1881.

Lady Alice, by William Allingham, page 115. *Songs, Ballads, and Stories*, 1884.

Lady Yeardley's Guest, by Margaret J. Preston, page 243. *Colonial Ballads, Sonnets, and other Verse*, 1887.

Lost and Found, by Hamilton Aïdé, page 176. *Rhymes and Recitations*, 1882.

Love-Child (The), by William Barnes, page 15. *Third Collection of Poems in Dorset Dialect*, 1863.

Mass for the Dead (The), by Sabine Baring-Gould, page 51. *Silver Store Collected from Mediæval, Christian, and Jewish Mines*, 1868.

Pearl of the Philippines (The), by Richard Henry Stoddard
page 117. *Poems,* 1880.

'Rajpût Nurse (A),' by Sir Edwin Arnold, page 238. *Lotus and
Jewel, containing ' In an Indian Temple,' 'A Casket of Gems,'
'A Queen's Revenge,' with other Poems,* 1887.

Revenge of Hamish (The), by Sidney Lanier, page 187. *Poems,*
1884.

Sir Richard Grenville's Last Fight, by Gerald Massey, page 8.
Poems, 1860.

Sister Mary of the Plague, by Eugene Lee-Hamilton, page 213.
Apollo and Marseyas, and other Poems, 1884.

Story of Naples (A), by Francis Turner Palgrave, page 68.
Lyrical Poems, 1871.

Willy Gilliland, by Sir Samuel Fergusson, page 21. *Lays of the
Western Gael,* 1865.

Winstanley, by Jean Ingelow, page 39. *A Story of Doom, and
other Poems,* 1867.

Woman's Love (A), by John Hay, page 64. *Pike County Ballads,
and other Pieces,* 1871.

Woodstock Maze, by William Bell Scott, page 96. *Ballads,
Studies from Nature, Sonnets, etc.,* 1875.

Young Princess (The), by George Meredith, page 230. *Ballads
and Poems of Tragic Life,* 1887.

INDEX OF FIRST LINES.

	PAGE
Above the pines the moon was slowly drifting	78
Against the long quays of Naples	68
All day unflagging in his stall	51
A sentinel-angel sitting high in glory	64
God makes sech nights, all white an' still	17
Had she come all the way for this	1
Here, in this leafy place	86
He said : ' The shadows darken down	227
I Catherine am a Douglas born	146
' I hear, Relempago, that you	117
I loved Hajarlis, and was loved	101
In her work there is no flagging	213
In the ranks of the Austrian you found him	13
It was three slim does and a ten-tined buck in the bracken lay	187
' Jessie, Jessie Cameron	59
Leon went to the wars	199
Now what doth Lady Alice so late on the turret stair	115
' Oh, never shall any one find you then ! '	96
On the sea and at the Hogue, sixteen hundred ninety-two	104
Our second Richard Lion Heart	8
Quoth the cedar to the reeds and rushes	39
' Seamen, seamen, tell me true	180

PAGE

Some miners were sinking a shaft in Wales 176
Still sits the school-house by the road 66
'Sweep up the flure, Janet 27
The conference-meeting through at last 57
The day is dead, the night draws on 126
The gift of God was mine; I lost 204
The king and his huntsman are gone to the chase . 247
The only son of the Count Lasserre 110
There's a living thread that goes winding, winding . . . 194
The sun is bright, the sky is clear 34
'T was a Saturday night, midwinter 243
'T was a wild mad kind of a night, as black as the bottom-
    less pit 80
'T was the body of Judas Iscariot 88
Up in the mountain solitudes, and in a rebel ring 21
'Wait a little,' you say, 'you are sure it will all come right' 140
When the South sang like a nightingale 230
Where the bridge out at Woodley did stride 15
'Whose tomb have they builded, Vittoo, under this tam-
    arind-tree 238
Yes, honey, you p'int'ly is purty 249

INDEX OF AUTHORS.

	PAGE
AïDÉ, HAMILTON	176
ALLINGHAM, WILLIAM	115
ARNOLD, SIR EDWIN	238
BARING-GOULD, SABINE	51
BARNES, WILLIAM	15
BROOKE, STOPFORD A.	247
BROWNING, ELIZABETH BARRETT	13
BROWNING, ROBERT	104
BUCHANAN, ROBERT	88
CHOLMONDELEY-PENNELL, H.	194
DOBSON, HENRY AUSTIN	86
DOYLE, SIR FRANCIS HASTINGS CHARLES	31
FERGUSSON, SIR SAMUEL	21
GORDON, A. C.	249
GUINEY, LOUISE IMOGEN	199
HARTE, FRANCIS BRET	78
HAY, JOHN	64
HORNE, RICHARD HENGIST	101
INGELOW, JEAN	39
KENDALL, MAY	227
LANIER, SIDNEY	187
LEE-HAMILTON, EUGENE	213
LOWELL, JAMES RUSSELL	17

	PAGE
MACDONALD, GEORGE	27
MASSEY, GERALD	8
MEREDITH, GEORGE	230
MORRIS, LEWIS	180
MORRIS, WILLIAM	1
PALGRAVE, FRANCIS TURNER	68
PAYNE, JOHN	126
PFEIFFER, EMILY	110
PRESTON, MARGARET J.	243
ROBINSON, AGNES MARY FRANCES	204
ROSSETTI, CHRISTINA GEORGINA	59
ROSSETTI, DANTE GABRIEL	146
SCOTT, WILLIAM BELL	96
STEDMAN, EDMUND CLARENCE	57
STODDARD, RICHARD HENRY	117
TENNYSON, LORD	140
THORNBURY, GEORGE WALTER	80
WHITTIER, JOHN GREENLEAF	66

University Press: John Wilson & Son, Cambridge.